THE NO LOVE LIKE GOD'S LOVE SERIES: BOOK 2

SHE NELL

ALL RIGHTS RESERVED. No part of this publication may be reproduced, distributed, or transmitted in any form or by any means, including photocopying, recording, or other electronic or mechanical methods, without the prior written permission of the publisher, except in the case of brief quotations embodied in critical reviews and certain other noncommercial uses permitted by copyright law. For more information, please contact the publisher.

Copyright © 2017 She Nell

Published by Light and Salt Press, LLC

Note: This is a work of fiction. Names, characters, places, and incidents either are products of the author's imagination or are used fictitiously. Any resemblance to actual events or locales or persons, living or dead, are entirely coincidental.

Light and Salt Press, LLC

8761 North 56th #290331

Temple Terrace, Florida 33687

Dedicated to:
You

And I, if I be lifted up from the earth, will draw all men
unto me.
John 12:32
King James Version

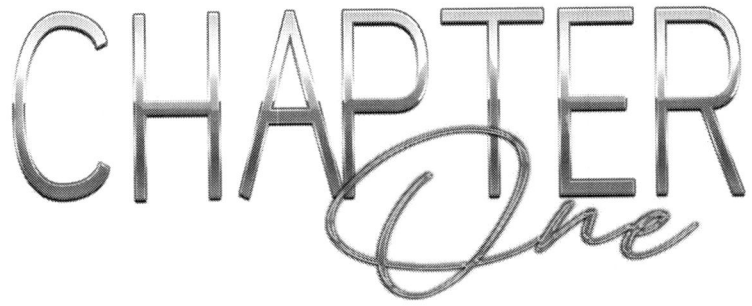

CHAPTER One

AS FLIGHT 331 floated over the dense clouds, Bryant stared out of the small, circular window. His bride, Chantel, slept on his shoulder as they flew from their island paradise back to the troubles at home. Bryant, being forewarned, had prepared a sermon for the morning, although secretively, he prayed that he would not have to use the words God had given him to say. He watched Chantel sleep, wondering if she would be ready to assume first lady duties if in fact Pastor Oaks did die. When he signed on to be the Youth Pastor at Christ Love Fellowship Church, he knew that one day he would take over as pastor. He did not want one day, to be this Sunday, however.

As the plane moved effortlessly above the ocean and clouds Bryant, could not help but wonder what God would have in store for him when he and his new bride landed in their hometown? He prayed fervently as the clouds passed underneath him. He fit all of the requirements for a good pastor. He possessed the best in education, leadership skills, his business degree, and experience. He had a strong foundation and he had grown up in church under his Pastor father and Pastor grandfather. Pedagogy was not his concern. He was well versed in church etiquette and protocol, and well-liked by many of the deacons. They were confident that if Bryant needed to be pastor of Christ Love Fellowship, he would be an excellent pastor.

Bryant, however, was not convinced that such an appointment would be a good fit. Several times, he'd sat in board meetings while the deacons and pastor, and he disagreed with them about operations. Several times, the deacons and Pastor Oaks dismissed programs that he wanted to start to help the community. He had even met resistance' starting the programs that were now very successful and thriving. Two of his ideas caused the church's size to increase by twenty five percent, and membership was steadily climbing. If you were to ask the deacons, they would credit the growth to the billboards and the television commercials that the church started doing when Bryant arrived. However, Bryant knew better. Knowing would not be good enough.

Chantel rested peacefully on her husband's shoulder. He assumed she was sleeping because her eyes were closed. She was thinking about all of the fun they had on the island and how she wished she could have stayed forever. She thought about the circumstances causing them to cut their honeymoon a week short. She knew that things would be completely different as soon as the plane landed at the airport. As it stood, they would land, get in a waiting car that would take her husband to the bedside of their ailing pastor and she to their home, which was formerly Bryant's home. There would not be the traditional act of being carried over the threshold, or the cat fight about removing furniture that looked too masculine into a house with a lady. They would be pushed into leadership as soon as the plane landed. Chantel nestled on her husband's shoulder, trying to savor the moment of just being Mrs. Bryant Taylor. She rested pleasantly for the duration of the flight, not being Pastor Taylor's Wife, future first lady Taylor, first mother of the church, or The Woman of God. For the entire flight she was just Chantel Taylor.

As the plane descended toward the runway, Bryant took Chantel's hand and kissed it gently. His warm smile filled her heart, and she knew she would love him forever. "Are you ready to do this?" he questioned with a sincere smile.

"As long as I am with you." She smiled back, secretly wishing that the phone calls never happened.

"Okay, well team Taylor; let's do it!" The plane landed and the flight attendants gave final directions.

As if on cue, they put on their game faces and held hands as they exited the plane. It was time to face whatever obstacle or challenge that would be thrown at the two of them. Determination set in as they walked off the plane and down to baggage pick up. Hand in hand, they were ready, or at least that was what they hoped.

They stepped out of the glass doors. Waiting with a black town car was Deacon Willis. He stood with a grimace and waited for Bryant to carry the bags to the car. Once Bryant placed the bags into the trunk, he opened Chantel's door in the backseat and then his own, next to her, as the round deacon wobbled around the car to the driver's side and sat behind the wheel of the car.

"Ya know that hood boy you got to join the church got shot, don't cha?" Before Bryant could answer, he continued. "Yeah, me and my Grace got in a bit of a shouting match over that thug. I told her just 'cause you like to do work with those types, that did not mean she should involve herself. I don't care how saved they lie to be."

"You mean try to be, deacon?"

"Naw, I mean lie to be. That boy ain't nowhere near righteous. He an ole thug, hood boy. You know that, Bryant."

Chantel sat listening to Deacon Willis. How could he be so judgmental? She could not understand. Just a couple of years ago, the Pastor had to pull him out of a bar as he drowned the misery of losing his wife in a bottle of brown liquor. Yet here he was, coming down on someone that was changing their life. She also did not like the fact that he called her husband Bryant instead of Pastor Bryant or Pastor Taylor. Furthermore, she was displeased with the assumption that Kingdavid was lying about changing his life.

"Yeah, they say they don't know who the shooters were. Just some random guys walked up to him asked him something, then opened fire. Crazy, probably asked him for drugs. You know those type of boys know how to get that dope." Deacon Willis finished as they pulled up to the home that Bryant and Chantel would share as husband and wife.

"Thank you Deacon. I will drive my car to see Pastor Oaks. I'll be right behind you," Bryant said as he hopped out of the passenger seat quickly to open Chantel's door and grab the bags.

He quickly put the bags near the front door and grabbed Chantel. "Wait a minute there, Mrs. Taylor." He stopped her from walking into the house. Swiftly, he picked her up and carried her over the threshold. "You didn't think I was going to let my bride walk into her new home without being, carried did you?"

Chantel smiled.

"I have to go, but I will be back as soon as I can, okay? Oh, and by the way babe, we are not throwing away my chair." He walked out of the door.

Chantel stood in amazement as he left. "I am loved like Christ loves the church," she said out loud, spinning around the room and falling back into the couch with a satisfied smile on her face.

The hospital was cold. Not normal, germ-killing cold, but a freezing at-death's-door cold. Bryant slowly approached the nurse's desk and ask for the room of Pastor Oaks. The nurse, occupied with her paperwork, did not look up, but she pointed to the left and said, "Room 205 on the end." Bryant thanked her. She did not respond. He slowly read the numbers and walked down the dim hallway until he reached room 205.

Pastor Oaks was in a private room with Mrs. Oaks by his bedside. She motioned for Bryant to come in. Only the blue light from the television lit up the tiny room. Tears began to form in Bryant's eyes as he looked at his sickly Pastor. Pastor Oaks had lost a lot of weight. His once muscular frame was mostly skin and bones. Mrs. Oaks looked like she had not slept for days. She motioned for Bryant to meet her in a corner of the room so that they could speak without disturbing the Pastor.

"Hey son, how was your trip back?" she whispered.

Bryant nodded, not taking his eyes off of Pastor Oaks, his mentor.

"He had a massive stroke and a heart attack a couple of days after you guys left. He has been here ever since. Bryant, the chances are not looking very good. Are you ready to preach Sunday?" She spoke in a straightforward tone. Still trying to keep from crying, Bryant nodded yes.

"Of course, he is ready," a raspy voice said. "Come over here now, son." The pastor extended his hand.

As Bryant slowly walked over to the Pastor's bedside, he grabbed his cold frail hand. "Son, my time may soon be over and I am okay with that, but I can't go without telling you, and you understanding that you are more than ready for this journey."

Bryant went to speak but the words were caught like a baseball in his throat.

"Son, what God has for you is for you, He will not and does not put more on you than you can bear. Promise me that when it is your time, you will step up and do as you know to do. You will do what is right according to the Word and vison of God. You will stand by our motto: Come ye all who are burdened and heavy laden. Lift up Christ. Son, promise you will do what is right." The pastor began coughing and closed his eyes. "Let me rest. I will see you tomorrow; tell the bride I said hello."

Bryant took a deep breath, said goodbye to Mrs. Oaks and somberly walked out of the hospital room toward the elevator. Once in the elevator as the doors closed and he was alone, Bryant leaned against the back wall and sobbed. As the doors opened, he composed himself long enough to get to his car.

He began to sob again. This time, his tears streamed from his eyes as if he were Jesus in the garden of Gethsemane. He decided to take the longest route home so his new bride would not have to see her king in a state of weakness. As he drove up to his home, he wiped his face with a tissue from the console of the car.

He regained his composure and brought his emotions back in check. He understood that he was a new husband with a beautiful woman waiting for him to open the door of their home. She was his good thing, and she would stand with him even through this tough trial that they would surely face together. The thought of not going through this season alone gave him some comfort. He did however, worry about the amount of transition that would take place over the year. He silently said a prayer and headed into the house.

A smile as wide as the great lakes came over Chantel's face as her husband walked into their home. She was taken aback by his smooth chocolate complexion every time he walked into a room. As he walked down the foyer toward her in the living room, she met him with a warm embrace. She noticed that his touch felt different. Something was upsetting him this evening.

"Baby, what is it?" she questioned in a soft gentle voice, leading him to sit down with her on the huge brown couch. He held his head down in disbelief about the words he had to tell her. He explained the Pastor's situation and what would happen if he passed away. He explained church protocol and the expectations that would be placed on them. He also explained the role Chantel would need to play as the leader of the women and his wife. After he explained, Chantel, being a woman after God's heart, whispered, "Baby, let us pray and ask God to lead us on which ever journey He choose for us, so that with His help we can handle everything that will surely be thrown at us." They bowed their heads, held hands and prayed.

CHAPTER Two

GRACE SMILED SWEETLY at the cleaning lady as she entered the dark room. A slight amount of light shone from the bathroom light that was left on in the small room. Grace sat in a hard brown chair reading, while Kingdavid rested peacefully in the hospital bed. The cleaning woman dry mopped the floor and gathered the trash quietly as to not to disturb the sleeping patient or his beautiful guest that had been at his side since he was brought to the rehabilitation center. She smiled at Grace and whispered about his improvement. Grace nodded and smiled. In her heart, she cried, but for the cleaning lady, a stranger, she smiled. As the cleaning lady finished and walked out, Grace took a slow deep breath and surveyed the sleeping Kingdavid.

She was so grateful that he had made it through the tragic experiences in his life. She knew that had the medic come a minute later, or the bullets shifted a little in one direction or another, she would be sitting at a cemetery instead of by his bedside. She said a silent prayer, thanking God for sparing the life of Kingdavid. He moved slowly as if in pain or discomfort and winced in his sleep. Grace gently rubbed his hand, thankful to be able to touch him. She remembered the phone call she received from Kimmee.

"Grace, it's Kimmee, King has been shot, and...... oh my God please help my brother!" Kimmee had said frantically. "They are taking him to the hospital!" she cried and hung up the phone as Grace raced to put on clothes and meet her at the hospital. Once there, she saw the crying Kimmee, who was covered in her brother's blood.

Grace automatically began to cry as she ran to embrace Kimmee. Loud wails came from their tiny frames as worry, fear and anxiety engulfed their spirits. Tears filled Grace's eyes as she remembered that night. The two women sat for what felt like an eternity as the hands on the clock slowly walked from one number to the next. They sat together holding hands, each saying a silent prayer that somehow by the grace of God, Kingdavid would make it. Several times they asked for update, and each time, the report was unfavorable. While the hospital staff did what they could to save Kingdavid's life, Kimmee went home to change and to pick up their mother and Grace went to the chapel.

Grace slowly walked into the small chapel on the bottom floor. Filled with hard wooden pews and stained glass of pictures of the country sides and oceans, the chapel was empty. She slowly walked to the front of the row of pews and sat down. With her hand covering her face she began to weep. Although she had not known Kingdavid for a long time, she was very fond of him. She felt that God was doing something wonderful in their lives. As Grace sat on the brown pew, she began to beg and plead for God to spare his life and to give him a second chance. She cried for his life, for his friendship and for justice. Grace sat in the chapel for an hour petitioning God. Once she ran out of words to say, ways to ask and scripture to recite, she went back to the waiting room. Once his surgery was complete, he was moved to the intensive care unit.

Bandages covered his chest and tubes cascaded from his mouth. Machines similar to the ones in his present room monitored his breathing, pulse, and blood pressure. He slept then as he did now, with Grace by his side as she had been since the shooting. Tomorrow was going to be a big day because Kingdavid was going to attempt walking. She stared at the wheelchair that sat over in the corner. She could understand why Kingdavid did not like the wheel chair and she was pleased that he was determined to regain his strength and walk. She was excited that he was eager to get better and live a normal life in Christ. She smiled again as her eyes examined his features.

He looked peaceful. His beautiful light-colored eyes were closed. His strong jawline was softened by his sleep. He did not look to be in pain. He was no longer worried about his attacker, justice or walking. He was at peace. She stared at him with loving eyes, blessing God in her heart for the chance to look at him sleep. Fear crept in her heart of losing him, and her eyes quickly filled with tears again. She batted her lashes to keep the tears at bay.

"What's wrong Gracie?" Kingdavid slowly opened his eyes.

"Nothing."

"Don't lie girl. I am okay. It takes more than a couple bullets to kill a King," he joked.

"It's not funny King ... You could have..."

"But Gracie I didn't," he said, cutting her words off and holding her hand. "I am going to be okay and soon back on the basketball court with my dude. I got to, for him and for you. I will Gracie, you will see I will." He spoke with determination in his weak voice.

Grace nodded. She sat back in the hard wooden chair and finished her book as Kingdavid drifted back to sleep.

As she sat, she noticed a buzzing sound coming from her tiny black purse that sat on the dresser near the wheelchair. She quietly walked over to her purse to retrieve her phone. She looked at the incoming call and frustration began to fill her body. She took a deep breath and looked back to ensure that she had not disturb the resting Kingdavid. Hesitantly, she walked out of the dark quiet room into the brightly lit busy hallway. Sitting on a nearby bench, she reluctantly called the number back. Her heart sunk to her stomach as her answered the phone with his heavy, agitated voice. She knew that she would have to hear words that she did not want to listen to at this time or at any time. Quietly she listened to her father explain that she was not a wife or for that matter a girlfriend to the young hoodlum that had been shot. Quietly she listened to the only man that had loved her until this day remind her that there was a possibility that this young thug she was running behind could have caused his own shooting. She listened as her only living parent told her that she was wasting her time running after a man that had a child with a woman he did not have the sense to marry. She listened silently as her hero told her that she would never be happy because that gigolo would always have a child or children we did not know about. She listened as her first love, her daddy, told her that her second love, Kingdavid, would never and could never love her.

While Deacon Willis believed that Kingdavid had gotten saved that day in the park, he did not feel he was saved enough to date, like, or love his only child. Deacon Willis was convinced that his daughter was destroying her life. He was determined to do everything in his power to make sure that he did not allow that to happen. He felt powerless on the phone as his daughter sat quiet listening to him rant for almost an hour. Although she listened, she still did so from the bedside of that whoremonger. The thought of the two of them probably laughing as he ranted made his flesh crawl. He told his daughter that she had to come home or that she would find herself without a home. She took a deep breath and agreed unwillingly.

She quietly walked back into the room where King rested. Slowly she walked to his bedside with tears in her eyes and a smile on her face. She pulled the blanket up over his chest. Gently she kissed his forehead and rubbed his shoulder. She hated to have to leave his side. She wished that she could stay until it was time for him to leave. She unfortunately did not have a choice, not knowing if her father's threats were empty. She headed out the door to her father's home.

As she pulled up to the large five bedroom estate, she parked her new Mercedes behind her father's Jaguar, which was parked behind the family's town car. She grabbed her small purse and headed up the cobblestone walkway into the grand entrance of the deacon's home. Placing her purse on the table that sat next to the French doors, she ran for the winding staircase. As she reached the first turn, her father called her name with his loud thunderous voice. Not wanting to argue, she listened until his insults were done and then ran to her room. As the door to her suite closed, she kicked off her shoes and fell helplessly onto her sofa. Grabbing her Bible, she decided only God could turn the heart of the king of her castle and make her queen to the King she desired.

Kingdavid sat in the wheelchair looking out of the window. Today he was determined would be the day that he walked. In his mind, nothing would be able to stop him. All week he worked at strengthening his body. Although he understood that he had a long road ahead of him he was anxious to get the process of full recovery started. His doctor explained that even if he did walk today, he would still need the aid of a cane for a while as he continued to rehab his body. A cane was something that Kingdavid felt he could deal with for a short time, but a wheelchair in his mind was unacceptable. He stared out of the window and prayed.

The cheerful nurse entered the dimly lit room. With a goofy smile and a childlike walk, she offered to push Kingdavid down the hallway to the exercise room. Kingdavid declined, choosing to wheel himself for what would be the very last time. Once in the room, he wheeled his chair up to the parallel bars. He took a deep breath and closed his eyes to pray. With his great upper body strength, he pulled his body up onto the bars. He stood for a moment. As he allowed his muscles and body to understand that they were standing, he prepared them to take a step. Slowly he brought one leg in front of the other and began walking the length of the bars. The nurse followed him every step of the way while the doctors stood by, cheering him to victory. When he reached the end of the bars, he slowly turned around and walked back to his waiting wheelchair.

"Now you just showing off. Get this man a gold-plated cane. He is the man now!" one of the other patients joked.

The entire room broke into laughter. Each of them was extremely happy that the youngest of all the rehab patients was recovering well enough to be headed home soon. Kingdavid wheeled back to his room with new excitement. He hopped back into bed and hid his cane in his sheets. He had a surprise for someone special.

The sound of Kingdavid's voice had Grace worried. She hung up the phone and raced down the stairs. She flew past her father so quickly, he could not question where she was headed. Once at the rehab center, she ran past the nurses to Kingdavid's room. She was shocked that his bed was empty and his wheelchair was gone. Panic filled her body and her heart began to race.

"Are you looking for someone Miss?" a voice said behind her. As she spun around, she could not believe her eyes. Standing before her was Kingdavid with a wide smile. She screamed and ran toward him. Embracing him gently, she kissed him softly.

"You are walking! That is so great, I am so happy, God is so good."

"Gracie, breathe."

"I can't help it. I can't believe it! You are up, you are up, God is so good, oh my God! King." She squealed and jumped up and down.

Kingdavid slowly walked back to the bed with his cane and sat watching as Grace praised.

Once her energy was almost completely drained, she sat in the hard chair she had made her altar many nights while waiting on Kingdavid to recover. She was relieved that he was better and thankful that he could walk again. Kingdavid explained that he would only be in the rehab center a couple more days before he would be released to go home. They both looked forward to starting a life and closer friendship together. Kingdavid wanted desperately to get out of the confined rehab center and into the world. Although one would assume that he had revenge on his mind, they would be sadly mistaken. In the forefront of his mind was seeing his son and starting a new life with what he hoped would be his girlfriend.

Kingdavid understood that they came from different worlds, but he felt that they were brought together for a purpose. Grace was on his mind consistently. He wondered about her heart's desires, if she had everything she needed, or if her day was going well. The only other person he concerned himself with to this level was his son. He loved and thought of his son all the time. Kingdavid never had these feelings for anyone. He did not feel that way about his mother, his sister, and not even Meka, the mother of his child and ex-girlfriend.

Kingdavid met Meka two years ago at a party. The two of them were drunk when they hooked up. After that night they started seeing more of each other and although it was never stated, they became a couple. Within the first year of their strange relationship Meka became pregnant and Kingdavid, not having a father, decided to always be there for his child. It had been a tough couple of years for the three of them, Kingdavid being in and out of trouble, Meka deciding to procure a career as a stripper, and their on again, off again relationship took a toll on the family unit. Kingdavid vowed to be a good father and that he was. He however was not in any way a boyfriend, lover, or friend to Meka. This made Meka a very hurt and bitter young lady.

CHAPTER Three

BRYANT STOOD in the mirror as he tied his purple tie into a trinity knot. His speckled tie matched the tiny purple boxes that covered his shirt. His navy pants complemented is tall frame. He wore dark brown shoes and a dark brown belt that matched his eyes. Chantel smiled, admiring him as she dressed. Chantel had decided that today was their debut as a couple and as possible new leadership. She thought it would be best to show everyone that they were a united unit from the start. Chantel wore a knee length purple dress with tiny navy flowers and navy shoes. A small navy sweater complemented the empire waist dress, and her two inch, strapped heels made her legs look flawless. She was his perfect complement, his rib, and his bride. She was Mrs. Bryant Taylor.

As they pulled up to the church, they noticed that the pastor's parking place was empty. Bryant looked at Chantel before deciding to park in his normal spot on the other side of the lot. He did not want the members to assume that he had a takeover spirit or that he was happy that their beloved pastor was dying. In fact, in Bryant's mind God was capable of doing anything including healing the pastor and restoring him to shepherd the sheep of Christ Love. He walked into the church with his bride on his arm and went to his office as they did before they were Pastor and Mrs. Taylor. Lorenz and Kimmee soon followed, giggling as they entered the office.

The four of them together was like old times. Just what Bryant needed before he had to face the church. He instructed Lorenz to start worship and asked Chantel if she would stay and pray with him before he went into the sanctuary. Once their prayer was finished, Bryant escorted Chantel into the sanctuary and she took her new seat on the front row. She left space for Mrs. Oaks out of respect; not because she expected her to show up. Lorenz finished singing his song about trusting God and the church was ready to hear from God through the man of God for the hour, Bryant. Bryant slowly walked to the pulpit and cleared his throat. He thanked the music minister and praise team for leading them into worship. He thanked the members for making their way out to the house of the Lord, and he thanked his wife for covering him in prayer, then he thanked God.

"He should've thanked God first," one of the older deacons whispered to Deacon Willis, who shook his head in agreement.

"If you would please turn your bibles to the beginning," Bryant said as the members looked around, then did as he instructed. He took a slow breath and allowed the Holy Ghost to speak through him. He told the church about beginnings and how God had a time and order for everything that was done. He explained that God's plans are not our plans, and His times are not our times. When he was done, there was not a member left sitting; everyone was up on their feet blessing the Lord. Every member shouted to glory; however several deacons and their wives looked around in wonder as they remained seated.

After the service, there was a long line of members wanting to shake Pastor Bryant's hand. Many of them were young people he had encountered while working the young adult ministry. Very few of the older members said much to him, although some did ask when Pastor Oaks would return. Bryant smiled politely at everyone, as did Chantel, who was by his side saying her farewells.

CHAPTER Four

AFTER SAYING goodbye to the members, Bryant and Chantel slowly walked to their car. They knew that the rest of the day would be trying on their hearts. They headed toward the hospital to visit Pastor Oaks. As they pulled into the parking garage of the hospital, the normally chatty Bryant was now quiet and very still. He gripped the steering wheel of the car while it ran idle. Chantel sat as well, understanding her husband's emotions and not wanting to rush him. He took a slow deep breath before looking into his wife's loving eyes. "You ready?" His heart was heavy with sorrow. Yet he had to pull strength from his Source.

"Yes," Chantel answered, not sure what she would see as she entered the room but wanting to remain strong for her husband. Bryant walked around the car to open her door. The two of them walked hand and hand out of the parking area and into the large hospital. They continued to hold hands as they rode the elevator to the 7th floor where Pastor Oaks had remained.

As the elevator opened, Chantel's body shook. "You okay?" Bryant questioned softly.

"Yes, just got a chill. That's all," she replied as she stared down the narrow hospital hallway.

"So you feel it too." Bryant's tone was somber. Her chill as she called, it was confirmation for what he felt. Death. They walked slowly down the narrow hall past rooms with beeping machines and sick people confined to hospital beds. As they passed each room Chantel tried her best not to look inside and stare or make eye contact with the patients. This hospital wing was very quiet compared to the afternoon traffic and noise that was outside. They walked quietly past the nurse's station until they stood in front of Pastor Oaks' room door.

His door, unlike many of the others, was shut. Bryant took a deep breath before tapping lightly. A weak voice told him to enter. He and Chantel entered the room and hid their fear behind warm smiles. Mrs. Oaks sat in a chair by the bed of her beloved. She no longer looked youthful and vibrant. Although she was still an attractive woman, it was easy to tell that this had taking most of her energy and all of her will. Her skin now appeared to have wrinkles and was dry. Her hair was pulled back tightly into a ponytail, and she wore no makeup. The women that often appeared to be younger than some of the young adults at church now appeared to be as old as some of the mothers of the church. The thoughts of her beloved crossing over to the other side could be seen in her eyes. The circumstance that had each of them standing around Pastor Oaks' beside were written on each forming wrinkles in her face.

Although Pastor Oaks tried to remain upbeat, it was apparent that he was not going to be with his beloved much longer. Despite the urges of his visitors to rest, Pastor Oaks insisted on giving instruction to Bryant. Bryant listened intently with tears in his eyes as Pastor Oaks told him everything he could about running Christ Love Fellowship Church. As if on cue, Mrs. Oaks asked Chantel to join her in the café for coffee. Chantel agreed and the two of them headed down the hall arm in arm to the café.

As they entered the café it was like walking to another world. They stepped out of the cold, stark hospital environment into the cozy, warm café that mirrored a downtown coffee house. Upon entering, their senses were filled with the warm aroma of fresh coffee and espresso. The décor of the café mimicked a cozy coffee lounge. It was filled with plush seating and shades of browns and bright blues covering the tapestry. Soft music played in the background as customers chatted about doctors and findings. Chantel and Mrs. Oaks stood in the short line and admired their surroundings. They each glanced at the chalkboard menu to decide what warm beverage they would lose themselves in and escape the issues that weighed heavy on their hearts.

With lattes in hand, they sat across from each other in plush caramel chairs with sapphire and slate-colored pillows confronting their weary bodies. They sipped their hot beverages in silence before stumbling to speak at the same time. Chantel conceded to her elder and allowed Mrs. Oaks to speak. Mrs. Oaks described what church leadership meant to women of God. She explained the differences between being a leader and the pastor's wife. Chantel nodded as she listened fully. Mrs. Oaks explained how important prayer would be to her life as well as her marriage.

"Honey, you have got to stay before the Lord and in your word if you want to make it in church business. The adversary is waiting for you to let your guard down so that he will be able to interrupt what God has for you. Many a man will come and try to take your husband's place. Be careful. Your husband is fine too. Like your pastor back in his day. The women will throw themselves at your husband, and or, they will secretly hate on you because they don't have what you have. So be mindful of who you entertain."

Mrs. Oaks took another sip of her latte and shared more wisdom with Chantel. As the attendants poured hot coffee into cups, Mrs. Oaks poured fresh knowledge into Chantel. She gave her instructions that she would need to follow in her absence. Once the pastor was gone and when Bryant was installed as the new pastor. Chantel listened, nodded and sipped her latte as she became full of new wisdoms. Chantel also shared with Mrs. Oaks her fears and concerns. The two spoke for over two hours as the perception of Godly women shifted to the realization of Godliness in a woman.

After finishing their lattes and conversation, they decided to leave the cozy atmosphere of the coffee house for the reality that they escaped hours ago. They walked up the dim cold hallway toward the elevator arm in arm. Once inside, Mrs. Oaks regained composure and put on a confident smile. Chantel followed along, positioning herself like the first lady. They stepped out of the elevator with a mask of confidence and walked down the dim lit hallway toward the room. They could hear laughter as they stood right outside the hospital door.

"Glad to see you are in good spirits. I truly hope you have not been overdoing it. You know the doctors said you need more rest. You are in here skinning and grinning; you should be taking it easy." Mrs. Oaks fussed as Pastor Oaks mimicked her and rolled his eyes.

Although he knew his days were short, he was not worried. He wore a crooked smile on his face as bright as the sun. He was determined to leave this earth cheerful and praising God. Before leaving, Pastor Oaks insisted that Chantel lead them in a word of prayer. Bryant held his wife's hand, shocked by the volume and power of the prayer that proceeded out of her mouth. Once she was finished, Pastor Oaks winked at Bryant, and the couple left the hospital forever changed and equipped for the journey that was ahead of them. They drove home in silence. It was obvious that they both had many thoughts running through their mind. As the tires slashed and a gentle rain fell, Chantel looked out of the window.

"Oh babe, I forgot to mention Kimmee says Kingdavid is coming home today. I think we should just give him a call and go to his house later in the week. That would give him time to get settled and readjusted. What do you think?" Chantel whispered, not wanting to disturb the peace of the silence. Bryant gave a nod to symbolize his agreement and they continued their drive home in silence.

CHAPTER Five

KINGDAVID SAT IN THE CAR, staring at the place where he almost lost his life. Visions of the night reappeared and played like a movie in his head. Two men, dressed in dark pants and hoodies, walked up to him, inquiring if he was banging Chantel. He was shocked and tried to explain that Chantel was like a sister to him and Kimmee. Then, pow, a fist to his face left him stammering from the blow. Regaining himself, he began to fight back. He skillfully fought both men and for a moment he had the upper hand. Then out of nowhere he felt fire and pain ignite his body as he fell to the ground. Screaming was heard as the two men ran away. A screaming Kimmee ran to him. He could not understand what she was saying. He saw her lips moving but did not hear a sound. He saw tears streaming down her face, but he could not hear. It was as if everything was moving in slow motion. He remembered seeing blue, red, and white flashing lights. His next memory was waking up in the hospital three days later.

"Are you okay? I can take you to Mama's house if you would like. I can understand if you would prefer not to be here. I can tell you that it has been pretty safe since that night. Nobody comes around. It would be nice to have you home, but

I can understand if you do not want to stay. I was hoping you would stay in the main house with me; that way you don't have to go up and down the stairs. Well, it's just two stairs, but that is better than all the stairs it would take to get to your place above the garage."

Kingdavid agreed, walked past the place where he once lay bleeding, and into the home he would share with his sister during his recovery. Kimme was happy to have her brother home and safe. She helped him into the house and then to the extra bedroom.

"Sis why does it smell like a man up in here?" Kingdavid questioned with a puzzled look on his face. "Don't look like you don't know what I am talking about. It smells like a dude has been here. Who you creeping with, Sis?"

"Boy please, ain't nobody creeping. Why are you in all my business anyway? Man, I swear little brothers do the most."

"So you admit that it was a dude up in here, huh Sis?" Kingdavid responded playfully.

"I am gonna admit it is none of your business. And I am gonna make us some dinner. How about that?"

"That is fine, but I am gonna find out, so you can tell me now or tell me later." Kingdavid laughed as Kimmee walked into the kitchen.

As they finished eating their dinner and joking, a gentle tap was heard at the door. Although the tap was mild, it still startled Kimmee, who had become jumpy after the shooting of her brother. They paused for a moment and looked at each other with concern. They were not expecting any visitors. Kingdavid slowly got up and crept toward the door as the light taps could be heard again. He opened the door with a stern look on his face, ready to defend himself from whatever was on the other side.

To his surprise stood a five-foot-seven beauty with golden highlights in her brown hair, and eyes that sparkled at the sight of him. It was the woman that stayed by his side while he lay in the hospital fighting for his life. Her smile set his pounding heart at ease, as well as his mind. He welcomed his angel into the house and into his arms. His embrace was firm and he needed this hug as much as she did.

She was happy to see him on his feet, walking, and able to eat, from the smell of the delicious meal that greeted her at the front door. He was now closer to being the boy she had begun to fall in love with month before the shooting. Kimmee welcomed her in and made a plate for her to join them at dinner. The three of them talked about the next steps for Kingdavid. He would need to recover fully before returning to work. Which meant he would be staying with his sister for a while. Although his own home was yards away, the group thought it would be better if he had someone with him full time. Kimmee worked in the daytime, but would be home every evening and Grace would come by in the daytime in between her classes and volunteering. Kingdavid, whose neck turned back and forth like a swing, watched the conversation between his sister and his heart's desire. Without consulting him, they had decided his fate and healing process for the next couple of months. Kingdavid smiled and wondered if this would be his life forever. He chucked to himself because he did not mind.

After the three of them ate, they watched a comedy before Grace decided it was time for her to leave her love and return to her father. She did not tell The Deacon, as she now referred to him, where she was going, only that she would not be long. "I don't feel like answering a ton of unnecessary questions," she groaned, "so I better head out now before I get too comfortable." She smiled, standing and gathering her purse.

"You know, once I kick King back to his place over the garage, it would be nice to have a roommate." Kimmee smiled eagerly.

"Naw naw naw; if she stays anywhere, it will be with me," Kingdavid interrupted.

"Now you know The Deacon ain't having that, and besides, I am not going to live with any man that I am not married to," Grace told the smiling Kingdavid.

"Who said you would be living with a man you were not married to?" Kingdavid grinned.

"Okay, we will talk about that later. Let's just get you well first," Kimmee interrupted. "Grace, thank you, and you are welcome to visit anytime. We should grab lunch and hang out one day soon." Kimmee followed Kingdavid and Grace to the door. The three of them exchanged hugs and Grace left to return home.

AS GRACE PULLED up the mini mansion, she noticed several of the deacon's cars parked outside. She wondered what the meeting would be about as she slowly walked into her home. She heard the heated conversation in the great room from the foyer. Although she tried to be quiet, her father heard her through the noise.

"Gracie, I see you made it home. How is your young thug, lil boogie, King Streetz, I believe they call him." Her father snarled.

"It's Kingdavid, Deacon, like the King David who God anointed, from the blood line of Jesus, who was God in the flesh," she schooled Deacon Willis.

"Girl, I don't care if his name was Messiah. He is still a thug and not good enough for you."

"Oh Deacon, don't you have company to see to?" She ran up the stairs to her bedroom suite.

Deacon Willis hung his head and walked back to his meeting. Several of the deacons were upset about the next course of action should the pastor of Christ Love Fellowship Church pass away. They knew that should this happen, Bryant would be installed as pastor. Although it was hard to change the rules, it was not impossible, and they were going to set out to do the hard thing. Many of them felt that Bryant would take the church in a different direction. Some felt that he did not understand the church's history and the way they did things at Christ Love Fellowship Church. Others thought that the new ideas and technology would make the church too worldly; therefore, if Bryant could not be controlled, he did not need to be the pastor over the flock. They needed someone who was able to keep the old saints of the church happy. Having a young person in a powerful position like pastor would mean that they would attract younger members, and that to them meant worldliness.

Grace, hearing their argument from her room, slammed her door shut and walked to the side of her bed. Grabbing her Bible from the nightstand, she read a verse and began to pray. Her cry filled the room. She prayed for her father's heart toward Kingdavid, she prayed for her pastor who was ill and possibly dying, and she prayed for Pastor Bryant, who was going to walk into a den of lions. She also prayed Kingdavid.

KINGDAVID SAT on the porch watching Kimmee drive off to work as the morning sun began to heat up the day. He was unsure of what his day would bring him. Wanting to avoid memories of his near death experience, he slowly headed toward the house. "Daddy!" a tiny voice said, causing him to turn around. "Daddy, you are o tay? Daddy," the tiny voice said, before the child jumped into his arms.

"Yes, Daddy is okay, but I still need to be careful, so I am gonna have to put you down." He placed his son onto the porch as he sat in a chair.

"I figure since you're home, I ain't got ta pay fo childcare. I'm gonna leave him her til I get back," Meka said.

"Okay, you ain't gotta beg me to take care of my son. Bye."

Meka rolled her eyes and walked back to her car. Driving off, she stuck her middle finger with its missing nail out the window and toward Kingdavid. He laughed and walked with his son into the house. The two of them ate cereal for breakfast, played video games, and ate hotdogs for lunch. They played all over the house, making a giant mess in every room. They were in the middle of playing monster when Grace knocked on the door.

The look she gave him was an easy indicator that Kimmee would be upset when she returned to the messy house. Kingdavid looked at the mess that they created and begged Grace to help them. He happily introduced her to his son as the three of them put Kimmee's house back in order. Just as they were finishing, Meka pulled back up to the house. She was very upset to see Kingdavid entertaining a lady.

"Come on Prince, let's go," she demanded, as the boy began to gather his things. "So dis how you get betta? You have some hoe up here playin' house and stuff wit my daggone baby? Boy, yo behind must be on dat good pain medicine, 'cause you thank that ish is okay. Dat ain't okay, King. Dat ish ain't okay, King!" she yelled, yanking the boy toward the car. Kingdavid did not have the strength to argue with her and he did not want to disrespect her in front of his son or Grace. He allowed her to carry on and then to drive away.

"So that was Princedavid and Meka, huh?"

"Yep," Kingdavid answered in a low voice.

Grace grabbed his hand and the two of them walked back inside of the house, both amazed by the theatrics they had witnessed. As they watched television, news about the ailing pastor came on the screen. They decided that they should pray for him together. They joined hands and took turns praying for their beloved Pastor and their church family.

CHAPTER Six

BRYANT AND CHANTEL rested in each other's arms as the scent of lovemaking and lavender candles filled the air. They slowly began drifting off to sleep before being startled by the ringing of Bryant's cell phone.

"Hello, yes, okay. Are you sure? It won't be a problem. Okay. We will be praying. Love you too." Tears filled Bryant eyes as he turned to his wife. He did not need to say a word; she could tell by the expression on his face that Pastor Oaks had died. They held each other once again and separately prayed for the strength to make it through what would be a very trying week.

Bryant stood at the pulpit Wednesday night praying before Bible study was to begin. He asked God for covering over the members of the Oaks family and for the members of Christ Love Fellowship church. Any babe in Christ could feel the tension in the atmosphere. There were rumors already starting about the direction of the church now that the pastor had passed. Some members supported Bryant and wanted to see him move the church into the next generation. They understood that times had changed, but God had not, and they wanted to help save as many people as they could. Others thought that Bryant and his ideas were against the traditional way of doing things. They felt that if God did not change, neither should they. After his much-needed prayer, Bryant began to teach the word of God.

Normally this would not draw complaints from members, because study was the reason for them attending the Wednesday night church service. Bible study with Pastor Oaks meant another Sunday service, except it was Wednesday. The praise team would sing, often leading into a spirit-filled worship hour, then he would preach a word similar to Sunday service with the church body shouting and dancing in the isle.

While this was entertaining, not much actual study was being done and members left hot, sweaty and unchanged. On nights like tonight, when Bryant was in charge of Bible study, it was a true study. He often had handouts with outlines and wrote things on a board. He encouraged members to take notes, and even gifted the men with nice notepads. Many of the members complained that it was like school and said that Bryant was too smart for his own good.

Those members did not hesitate to tell the deacons of their displeasure during the wake for Pastor Oaks on that Friday. They secretly spoke in between the service as people gathered to speak good words about the deceased Pastor. They whispered as the groups of friends and family came in to pay their last respects. Bryant and Chantel, knowing that all of this was going on, focused their attention on helping Mrs. Oaks and doing the will of God. After making sure she was home with family that evening, they drove to their house to get prepared for what would be an emotional day.

The service for Pastor Oaks was held at Deeper Fellowship Church, a mega church that sat over 2,000 people. The church had a massive gallery area, where members past and present gathered, waiting for the ushers to let them into the giant sanctuary. Once inside, Bryant, Chantel, and other members of leadership sat in the front row of the church.

Surrounded by family and friends of the Pastor, they held their composure and waited for the service to start. Kingdavid slowly walked up to the microphone with his head down. He made eye contact with Grace, who offered him a sweet smile and nod of approval.

"What's Thug Life doing up there?" Deacon Willis questioned in a loud whisper to Grace, who was sitting on the row behind Bryant and Chantel with her father. "Why is he up there? This is not a rap concert. Lawd please don't let him make a fool out the church," he continued.

"Daddy," Grace scolded her father, "just watch and hush for the sake of Pastor Oaks, God rest his soul." She gave another warm smile to Kingdavid.

Kingdavid smiled at her and was instantly calmed. He took a deep breath and began to sing without music or interruption, the Lord's Prayer. Tears fell gently from the eyes of those in attendance as he passionately sang each verse. The absence of music did not change the beauty of the song. His voice was smooth as silk, each note perfectly followed the one before, and it cut to the soul of even Deacon Willis. Deacon Willis sat with his mouth open and his eyes fixed on Kingdavid. He had not heard the Lord's Prayer sung since his late wife sang it for him the Sunday before she died. He was astounded by Kingdavid's ability. Once he was finished, Kingdavid released the microphone and walked down to his seat on the opposite side of the church.

"I still don't like him; anybody can sing. The devil was the leader of the praise team. He still is a thug. That display means nothing. Plenty of children can sign the ABC song and can't tell you one letter of the alphabet. Just because you can sing the Lord's Prayer does not mean you know the Lord," Deacon Willis whispered to Grace. "Do not shhh me young lady, that boy ain't nothing but trouble and he has the bullet holes to prove it. Why you would want to involve yourself with that type of element, I do not know. You know good and well you were not raised that way. Your poor sweet mama is probably in heaven talking to Pastor Oaks about it right now."

"She is talking about one of us daddy, but I am sure it is not me," Grace whispered. "Now please stop and enjoy the service," she finished, looking straight ahead at the speaker. She had shut Deacon Willis down, and he admired her for being the only other woman besides his late wife that could. He could not bear the thought of losing Grace also. If he had to let her go, it would not be to some poor thug that was playing church. Although the service could have lasted half of the day, it was over within an hour and a half. After the burial, the guests gathered at Christ Love Fellowship for the repass.

Several of the members told Bryant that they enjoyed the direction of the church and that although Pastor Oaks was going to be missed, they were pleased he would be leading. Bryant smiled, not thinking it was the proper time to discuss church business. However, Bryant was the only one with those feelings.

"Bryant, let me speak to you for a minute son," Deacon Willis said, "over here." Bryant followed. "Thank you son," Deacon Willis said. "Look, I know that it's still early in the day but I hope you have your sermon planned for tomorrow." Bryant nodded as he sipped his drink.

"Good, good, now this study you are doing on Romans is great, but you need to make sure you always put something in there about finances. You see, we can't run if we can't make money son. There is church and then there is church business. Church business includes making money for the lights, the building, everything. Your salary included. So unless you and that pretty bride of yours want to live on the street, you need to put a word in about God blessing those that give to the church.

That way they won't stop giving, and if you are real good, they will give more. Do you understand what I am telling you boy? You need to make them feel like if they do not give, God won't deliver them. Don't give me that look; you know that we have to be out of this building in six months and ain't no way for that to happen if we don't have money. So you best start making them feel as if they need to give, or you and yours and me and mine will be in the street. I don't know about you, but God did not call me to live a poor man's life." Deacon Willis adjusted his expensive suit jacket and walked away.

    Bryant stood silently thinking about what the deacon had said to him. The deacon was right about one thing: they had exactly six months left to leave their building and find another. He had heard messages on money, some by Pastor Oaks, and he knew that they brought in extra funds. People in need of a blessing would often give their last dime if the man of God said that it would get them out of bondage. But Bryant believed the price of freedom from the chaos of this world could not be paid for with manmade money. He knew that the only way to escape was to give God the most expensive possession we owned, our hearts. Money would not change a situation; only giving your heart and life to Christ could do that. Bryant sipped his drink once more as Deacon Willis and the other Deacons eyed him. Deacon Willis was assuring the group of men that things were going to be okay and run smoothly. Bryant knew that things were going to be anything but smooth. He did agree, however, that things would be okay.

CHAPTER Seven

BRYANT SAT at his desk in his office. He was in his second favorite place in the entire church, to the first was the altar. He sat in his chair rocking slowly back and forth, thinking about his new position. He was in two hours to be confirmed as Pastor of Christ Love Fellowship Church. He sat in same office not wanting the bigger office that was once his mentor's office. To Bryant, a couple of feet and a slightly bigger desk did not make much difference. He was comfortable in his office. It was where God met him as he studied and meditated on the word. It was where God had told him Chantel was to be his bride. It was also where God had commanded him to make a radical choice that would shake the foundation of the church. He sat slowly turning in his chair as he looked at the bookcase and the many books. He smiled as he looked at the pictures of Chantel and himself. She was his rock. When he told her what the plan would be, he thought for sure that she would not understand. Although she was puzzled at first, Chantel gained full understanding after he explained every detail. She was okay with his decision and grateful to have him as the overseer of the church and her home. Everything was set in place. The only other people that needed to be told were arriving shortly for the service. He knew that it was customary to tell the deacons first, but he thought it would be best and less room for error if they found out with everyone else. He aware of the deacon's secret meetings. He was certain that if he listened to God, it would work out and this was the first step, one that would surely shake the bedrock of the church. Telling the deacons would be giving them a head start on their plotting and he was not in the habit of showing his hand early.

He sat rocking in his chair, going over his notes for the sermon he was to deliver. This would be the first sermon he would deliver as the Pastor of Christ Love Fellowship Church. The message that God have given him was about trusting God. He would need to trust God more than ever as he prepared to say words never heard in Christ Love Fellowship church. He smiled as Chantel, Lorenz, and Kimmee walked into his office as they customarily did prior to him becoming Pastor. The group laughed and joked until the other members began arriving.

Ten minutes before the start of service, Lorenz walked in the sanctuary and sat at the keyboard. Bryant had requested worship music and Lorenz delivered with a soulful ballad of worship and prayer. As he played, Bryant escorted Chantel, the first lady of Christ Love Fellowship Church, into the sanctuary. She sat on the first row next to Kimmee and the mothers of the church.

Across from them sat the deacons, some with smiles, others not impressed with Bryant or his entrance into the sanctuary. Bryant sat behind the pulpit while Lorenz continued to sing. Bryant was grateful for his friend, because this time he was ministering to the uncertainty in Bryant's heart. Bryant knew that God would continue to provide, however, he was certain that there would be backlash where there need not be backlash. As Lorenz finished playing, Deacon Willis came to the microphone to deliver a prayer. Once prayer was over, Bryant slowly walked to the pulpit.

"Brothers and Sisters, it is an honor to stand before you today as the Pastor of Christ Love Fellowship Church. I am humbled beyond measure that God would entrust me with such a task to be the overseer of his people. I am blessed by so many of you and I thank you for trusting the God in me. That being said, church you know that we have six months left in this building and it is our desire to get in a larger building of our own."

The members of the church shouted Amen and clapped.

"That being said, church, I am requesting that instead of getting a salary from the church, the church take my salary and put the entire thing toward the building fund for the purchase of a new building. I am also asking other paid members to prayerfully considering putting their pay toward the building fund."

Lorenz and the janitor were the only paid members to clap and support their new pastor. "Church I can't speak for anyone's pockets. I can only do what God has requested of me," Bryant continued, as he noticed several of the deacons whispering and looking at Chantel. "I understand that you must talk to your families, and most of all pray. As for me and my house, I have been a successful freelance writer, as well as a ghostwriter for some pretty big names. I am sure that God will continue to see my wife and I through as she takes time off of her job to finish up her college degree." The women clapped and smiled. They were happy that Chantel would be completing her dream.

After Bryant's announcement, he prayed and God used him to preach his word. Sweat poured from his face as he brought forth a passionate word. Several of the men were filled with the Holy Ghost and began to leap out of their seats. Women caught up in the sprit ran and shouted for the glory of

God. Lorenz was in tune and his playing was perfectly ordained for the message on trust. The atmosphere in the church was vibrant. As if a refreshing wave had roared through the church, the members were saturated in the presence of God. After the word was delivered, Kingdavid took the microphone and began to sing. His voice filled the room and intertwined with the atmosphere. God spoke through his song, healing those that were ill, and delivering those that were bound.

The church service lasted its normal hour although time seem to stand still during the service. Once alter call was done, Bryant and Chantel went to the entrance of the church to shake hands with members as they left. The members smiled and spoke about how they were blessed by the message. Some of the Deacons walked by without saying a word while others reminded the new pastor that they had a meeting Tuesday at ten in the morning "sharp". Bryant smiled and nodded as he tended to the members.

BRYANT ARRIVED at the church at nine o'clock for the ten o'clock meeting with the deacons. He sat in his office and prayed before gathering his things and walking to the conference room. He made a small pot of coffee for the deacons and himself. Bryant was as ready as he could be for the meeting. As the deacons began to file in, they got cups of coffee and greeted each other before sitting down.

"Will your wife be taking on secretary duties now that you have forced her off her job Pastor?" Deacon Marshal asked.

"No, she will not. That reminds me. We need to find a new church secretary," Bryant answered.

"Ain't nobody going to work for free!" Deacon Jones shouted, glaring at Bryant to show his dissatisfaction.

"Deacon Miller, will you head up the search for a new

secretary?" Bryant said. "Now I know it came as a shock to some of you, but I am serous about my salary going to the building fund. Deacons, we need to get out of this building. God has so much in store for this church. I am not going to tell you what to do, but I am going to ask you to really pray about it. Several of you are taking a salary from the church for various things."

The deacons looked around at each other mumbling.

"Next, order of business is the search for a youth pastor. Are there any candidates?"

No one answered.

"Okay, seeing that there aren't any, we need to do a diligent search and pray. Deacon Owens, will you head up the search?"

Deacon Owens nodded.

"Thank you, sir." Bryant ran the meeting smoothly. The deacons conformed to Bryant style and expectations although they did not want to conform.

After Bryant's meeting he locked up his office and headed home. In the parking lot, Deacons Willis, Jones, and Marshal stood having a conversation about the meeting. They threw up their hands to wave goodbye as Bryant drove away. They wore fake smiles until his car was no longer in sight. Then they completed their conservation. It was obvious to Bryant who his enemies would be throughout this transition, but he remembered that his enemies were to be his footstool. Bryant smiled as he drove home.

"Something must be done," Deacon Jones said. "He is going to have our church full of riffraff; watch my words. Bunch of young people with phones and labtops," he continued.

"You mean, laptops," Deacon Willis corrected him.

"That is what I said, labtops; anyway they going to be all in the church with jeans on, drinking in the sanctuary, you know I am right Marshal."

"Whatever we do," Deacon Willis started, "we need to

make sure it works. We cannot give him room to turn it around for his good. If we are going to take him down, we need to make sure that he is down for good and unable to bounce back," he finished.

They stood for a couple moments more making sure that they had an outline of their plan. They agreed that although he was a nice young man, he was not the right fit for what they had done with the church. They were accustomed to running the church in a manner that had been effective for a number of years. Having a young minster come in with new ideas and new systems was not something they wanted to embrace.

To the deacons, Christ Love Fellowship did not need a basketball ministry, and all of these teen and young adult trips were not needed and took money away from them. After their outside parking lot meeting, they each got into their expensive cars and headed to their lavish homes.

As Bryant pulled up to his home, he saw his bride on the porch speaking to Kimmee. He greeted the ladies who were speaking about Kingdavid's voice. They spoke of how his song shifted the atmosphere and ushered in a fresh anointing. Bryant agreed that Kingdavid had a gift and he could have a future in music.

CHAPTER Eight

KINGDAVID TINKERED with his car while singing an Anthony Evans song. He matched every note perfectly. It was hard to tell were Anthony stopped and Kingdavid began. Their voices blended seamlessly. He was excited to feel well enough to tinker with his automobile. He knew that it would be very soon that he would need to start to drive again, and he was eager to get back on the road.

As he tinkered, a black car pulled up in the driveway and two men in suits stepped out of the car. They walked toward him and he could feel the nerves in his body tingle. The last time strangers approached him he spent weeks in the hospital and almost lost his life. This time would be different. If need be, this time he would shoot first. He put his hand in his pocket where he hid a small pistol.

"Can I help you?" he questioned the men as they stepped closer.

"You the one they call Kingdavid? We are from Deca, the Music label. We have been looking for you since the funeral of my uncle," the taller of the two men said.

"Who's your uncle?" Kingdavid questioned with a smirk.

"Come on man, Pastor Oaks, look, we not here to start

anything, so you can ease up off that lil pistol in your pocket. Ya feel me. We, well I heard you sing at the service and I told my partner bout you. Was hoping we could do business. I am Ralph and this is Darren. We are the CEO's and producers of Deca Music. We are interested in you putting out a couple singles and if it does like I think it will, a few albums. That is if we all agree."

"For real?" Kingdavid questioned. He was shocked that this was happening now after the many years he tried to break into the business. Now, as he stood tinkering with his car, he was offered a music deal.

"Yeah, if I like your sound. Sing something," Darren said, waiting to be blown away according to what Ralph had told him.

Kingdavid dropped his cleaning rag on the hood of the car and began to sing. His smooth voice began to float over the wind and take off towards for the heavens. All at once the atmosphere shifted from a calm day of tinkering to a place of worship. Ralph began to sway as Kingdavid sang. Darren looked toward the ground with his ear toward Kingdavid's voice. Kingdavid sang. When his song was over, he looked at the two men who stood in his yard speechless.

"Man, if you want this like we want it, meet us up at the studio on MLK at six pm," Darren said without hesitation.

"Okay. Thank you man," Kingdavid said, trying not to smile too big.

"See you then," Ralph said, and the two men got in the car and drove off.

Kimmee could not get in the door fast enough before Kingdaviv began explaining to her and Grace, who had come over and was forced to wait to hear the news. He shouted the news so loud it eclipsed the sounds of the girls squeals of excitement. The three of them jumped up and down, ran and praised. Excitement filled the tiny house. It was so full of energy that it whisked them out of the door and to a local restaurant to celebrate over dinner.

DECA MUSIC WAS LOCATED in a small building surrounded by houses and local stores. Many people drove by the Music Empire all the time without knowing that that is where some of the very songs they danced to came from. Kingdavid was shocked that they would be starting a gospel label and he was overjoyed to be the first gospel artist on the Deca Music imprint. He was a fan of some of the secular projects they put out in the past, but he had not listened to too much of the music lately. His appetite for music had changed since he accepted Christ. It was not that he did not listen to secular music; he did from time to time. He was however mindful of the message that the songs gave, and he preferred gospel.

He walked into the dimly lit office space and was instructed to sit and wait. He looked at the pictures and autographs that lined the walls. He wondered if one day his gospel album would be there. He pictured himself doing collaborations with gospel rappers, shooting videos and accepting Dove Awards. He smiled as his fantasy played out before him. Ralph came in, breaking up his fantasy. After offering him something to drink Ralph took Kingdavid into the office.

The lavish office was huge and just next to it was the studio where hits where made, according to Darren, who had just joined the two men.

They took turns explaining to Kingdavid that he had a two single deal. He was to record two singles and if they did well, he would be offered a deal for an entire album. Kingdavid was excited to get started and the team had the first song already picked out. They gave him a copy of the music and he read over the lyrics. He read them twice before speaking.

"What's wrong?" Ralph said, noticing the look of concern of Kingdavid's face.

"Nothing, it just I'm looking for the worship in the lyrics. There is no mention of God or Jesus. Not even implied," Kingdavid answered.

"Well no, but it's not a bad song. It's a love song, and God is love so there you go. It will be able to cross you over from gospel, only to the new vibe. We call it positive music. See it's not good ole gospel, but it's not bad; it's positive. Come on, what you say? You can make a lot of money and when we get your album deal. You can put one gospel song on that. What do you say man, this is a once in a lifetime kind of deal. What are the chances of another music label coming into your church and hearing and offering you a chance like this? Dude, this must be God. At least that's what we believe. What do you say?"

Kingdavid thought for a moment. It wasn't a bad song. It would give him a bigger audience, and a better platform. Besides, Ralph was right, what were the chances of something like this happening again? "Okay," he said, and the three of them went over into the studio.

Night after night, Kingdavid would find himself in the studio late, recording and rerecording the single. His voice was in excellent shape and sounded wonderful over the microphones. Each night he would belt out his tune until it was perfect. The late nights began to catch up with him and cause him to be late to church service more often than usual. Kimmee did not nag in the beginning but soon began to complain that Kingdavid was out all night and sleep all day. Grace complained also, because they did not see each other as much due to the recording sessions. She informed Kingdavid that the once full church had seemed to be thinning with membership lately. Kingdavid promised that he would attend with Grace next Sunday.

CHAPTER Nine

KINGDAVID PARKED his car into one of the many spaces available in front of the church. As he looked at the spaces in the parking lot, he was taken by surprise. As someone who used to work the parking lot ministry, he was shocked at the number of cars missing from church. He looked at his phone to check the date. Today was Young Adult Sunday, one of the Sundays that normally brought in record numbers of people. However, on this Sunday there were not many souls in attendance.

As he walked into the church he spotted Grace as she sat in the middle row of chairs looking back at him and smiling. She motioned for him to join her and he quickly sat next to her. Deacon Willis flared his nostrils across the room, staring at the two of them smiling at each other. He was not pleased with the budding relationship. His daughter was old enough to make her own decisions, however he felt he had the right to tell her which ones she needed to make. Dating the church thug was not one of the ones she needed to make.

Although the congregation was thinner than Bryant would have liked, that did not stop him from delivering a word that changed hearts and taught the believers how to overcome. As the deacons sat with their arms folded and scowls on their faces, Bryant taught the saints as the Lord had instructed him. There was little to no jumping around the church. There was no shouting, just a quiet wave of the hand and an occasional amen. Lorenz ushered in a sweet sprit of worship as he played. The atmosphere was set, the word was brought forth and lives were changed.

When it was time for alter call a few people got up for prayer, but no one joined the church. The deacons began to mumble toward one another as Bryant, still cheerful, gave the benediction. Members could be overheard complaining about the leadership, saying that during the time of Pastor Oaks the church was packed. Although the music had not changed they complained as if it had changed.

The deacons that counted the money left and returned at lighting speed after the service with disappointment on their faces. The offering was enough to take care of bills and pay the pastor's salary toward the building fund. There was not enough for deacons to take their normal share for counting. Although this was not how most churches did things, it was customary for Christ Love Fellowship.

The deacons looked at Bryant as if he was the antichrist. This young man, in their opinion had come in and disrupted the church. Frist it was the Young Adult outings. Then it was a host of new projects and ministries, some they managed to stop, like the basketball ministry. Now, he was asking the church to put his salary toward the building fund. The deacons felt that he was changing too many things and those changes caused membership to be at a low. A few deacons believed in Bryant, but they were outnumbered.

Grace waited for Kingdavid to speak to Bryant before she gave him a friendly hug and grabbed his hand. She did not care that some of the deacons and mothers of the church were looking and frowning. She was happy that Kingdavid had made it back to church and that she was able to see him in person.

Although they made it a point to speak nightly, there was nothing that could compare to a face to face interaction.

Kingdavid missed her as well, and he gently pulled her close as they walked by their cars. He whispered his love in her ear. She blushed like a schoolgirl and giggled. They wouldn't tell anyone, but it was easy to see that they were in love. Deacon Willis shot daggers with his eyes from across the parking lot. The last thing he wanted was for his only child to be caught up with someone like Kingdavid. Deacon Willis lowered his head in disappointment, walked to his car and drove away.

Still bundled together, Kingdavid and Grace decided to have lunch with Pastor Bryant, Chantel, Kimmee and Lorenz at the pastor's house. Once there, the group had a deep conversation about the things going on in the church. They comforted Bryant, who was concerned that the loss of members was his fault. They reassured him that God had a plan and that everything was going to work out for his good and the good of the church. Before leaving, Kimmee and Lorenz agreed to go to Kingdavid's show on Friday. Although he was not singing gospel, they still wanted to support their family and Grace, who would otherwise have to sit alone.

Chapter Ten

GRACE FELT out of place in her boyfriend jeans and *Jesus is my Jam* t-shirt. Although her ankle heeled boots were very cute and her hair and makeup was flawless, she wore more clothes than the average concert goer. She looked at Kimmee who was dressed similar to her, and then to the crowd of skin. Most girls wore short dresses that clung to their bodies. Some wore shorts that stopped just below their butts and heels at least six inches or more. She knew that Kingdavid did not sing gospel, but she did not think he would attract this type of crowd.

The venue was filled with mostly women, gay men and reluctant boyfriends, forced to come to the show. The reluctant men seemed to be pleased once they entered to the venue and saw the amount to flesh that walked before them. They tried not to seem as if they were staring as half-dressed women pranced by, some even brushing up against them flirtatiously.

The lights turned off and on, signaling to the guests that they should be seated. The group went to the front row where they were to be seated among the fans. Kimmee was happy to see so many fans chanting Kingdavid's name. She smiled, proud of his success and even prouder to be his lady. Kimmee was excited too; her brother was going to make it! The lights went down and Kingdavid walked out on the stage.

Once the lights came up, he was center stage, surrounded by barely clothed dancers and the beat dropped. He began dancing sexually with each of the dancers as he covered a mashup of three of R. Kelly's songs. He slid his body across the stage, grinding as if he was making love to someone and stuck his tongue out, wiggling it to the sounds of screaming women. Sliding his body up to a standing position, he humped the air as women jumped and screamed.

Grace stood. Tears filled her eyes as disappointment covered her face. Her heart tore. She hated to think it but, what if deacon daddy was right? The woman behind her took off her panties and tossed them on stage. Grace became sick to her stomach. She looked over toward Kimmee and Lorenz, who stared as if they were caught in a trance. Kingdavid's voice echoed throughout the venue, but it was not the same voice she was used to. When she overheard one of the ladies describe all the vile things him she had enough. She pushed through the crowd with Kimmee and Lorenz behind her. They drove home in silence. No one knew what to say or think. The show was too much for them all to bear.

"Why did you leave early?" Kingdavid questioned Grace over the phone early the next morning. "You didn't even hear me sing my song, Gracie. Y'all just left. What was with that? I thought you of all people would support my dream and success." Kingdavid was filled with disappointment.

Grace stared at the phone as if a stranger was on the other end of the receiver. Shaking her head, she could not believe what she had just heard. "King, honey," she started slowly, "Babe look, I support you singing, but I am not supporting you grinding on strange women or on the ground. I am not supporting women professing that they are ready and willing to have sex with you or tossing their nasty panties on stage. Now you said that you love the Lord and that you were gonna use your God-given talent to glorify the Lord. You did not glorify God, King, you glorified sex and all the things of the world. I thought, I thought, I do not know what I was thinking. King I am not sure if we are going to work. I can't be unequally yoked, I just can't. If this who you are going to be that is fine. You are just gonna need to be you without me," she said sadly.

"Grace, wait. You don't understand. I do love God; I do want to sing for Him. The label said I just have to do this to build up my fans, that's all. I have one single now, but if I build up my fans and prove I can sell, then I can sing what I want. It is part of the process Grace, please. Please Gracie baby listen to me. I promise, I haven't changed; that was just for the show. I don't care about them women. I love you, Grace. Please listen."

"I know you love me King. My question is, do you love the Lord? How can you say you love Him, then have sex with the stage, condone women wanting to do vile things with you, dance and grind on women? Is the fame worth it?"

"Come on Grace that's not fair. You know I never got in this for the money. I love to sing. It's my gift from God and I love using it."

"Yeah, well not for nothing, you sound good but not the same. You say that you have a gift from God, but you don't use it for his glory, King."

"Grace, this is a chance of a lifetime. This is my chance to get fans, so I can get signed, and sing what I want to sing."

"You need to read John 12:32. Look I got class in an hour. I hope it works out, King. I gotta go. Bye." Grace looked at the phone after she hung up. Her heart tore a little more.

"Who you given scripture to baby?" Deacon Willis said as he walked past her on the steps.

"No one daddy, where are you going?" she asked.

"Church meeting sugar, I'll be back," Deacon Willis said as he walked out of the door.

Grace walked behind him to head to her class.

Chapter Eleven

BRYANT SAT at the long oak table in the conference room silently, praying to God that this meeting would go well. Although he sat at the head of the table, he did not feel much like the head of anything. The deacons came into the room one by one, some speaking and others not saying a word. Each dressed as if this was a Sunday service, while Bryant wore a green polo style shirt and beige colored slacks. Bryant sat tall in his chair so that he would not seem out of place. Once the deacons were seated, the roll was called and the meeting began.

Topic one was the lease on the current building. According to the leasing agreement, the church need to be out of their current building in a couple of months. The relocation committee had several locations picked, but only one sparked the interest of most of the board. Pastor Bryant could overrule the board, but he did not think that would be a wise idea. They were in agreement that the location would allow them to grow but they had a dispute about how to get the extra money needed for the down payment.

Several of the deacons felt that even if they could get the down payment, they would not have enough income to maintain the coast of running a big facility. This was also Bryant's concern. Since he had taken over, the church membership saw a dip. Services that were normally at capacity now sat only a hundred or so people. Bryant was very discouraged, and it showed on his face.

"Well Brother Treasurer, how much do we have toward the move saved?" Deacon Willis asked, fully aware of the amount of money in the bank.

"Brother Willis," Deacon Jones began, "it appears that we are short in that department. We are missing some funds."

"How can that be? Last we counted, we had enough, unless someone is going in the funds and taking unaccounted for money?" Deacon Marshal questioned, as he and the three deacons looked at Bryant.

"What?" Bryant asked, shocked that they would look his way. "I do not have anything to do with the money. In fact, I don't even take what I am owed. That goes straight to the church. I am uncertain why you would look in my direction."

"Just because you don't ask for your money doesn't mean you don't take your money," Deacon Jones said in an accusatory tone. "How else are you paying for that house, and did I hear your wife came off her job? Yet, she is always in a new dress and shoes. How else you getting the money?"

Bryant sat back in his chair with his mouth open and his eyes steaming towards the deacons. He could not believe what he had heard. The very men that once mentored and congratulated him now sat before him accusing him of stealing.

"Do not just sit there boy, answer the question?" Deacon Marshal yelled.

"Now Marshal, you can't just bombard someone like that. Give him a minute," Deacon Miller interjected. "It's okay son, just answer the question."

"First of all, what we are not going to do gentleman is speak in an ill light about my wife, ever! Now as I have stated before, I make a great living as a writer and do not need to take the churches money to pay my bills or handle my responsibilities. Which include my wife. So if there is any question as to where the money is going, I suggest you look among yourselves because you all have access to the money. I do not!" Bryant wanted to leave but knew it was in his best interest to stay.

"Well, well brother, I must offer an apology. It seems there was a counting error and we have more than enough," one of the other deacons said after looking back over the paperwork. "Brother Pastor, please accept my apology. I meant no harm, just wanted to make sure the house of the Lord was taken care of. You can understand that, I am sure."

Bryant did not say a word. He looked at the deacons in disgust. The meeting continued without incident, although the conversation did elevate from time to time about the direction of the church. The deacons as a whole felt that Bryant was doing a good enough job but that he could do better. They blamed that lack of attendance on the lack of billboards and commercials for the church. Something about doing those types of things did not sit well with Bryant's heart.

They argued back and forth about the benefits of advertisement. Bryant was still not convinced and he refused to do any ads or take pictures for promotional purposes. He maintained that the church was not about him but about God, and that he did not deserve to be lifted up for all the world to see as they drove on the highway. The deacons disagreed and began speaking about the success and money billboards brought into the church.

Still not wanting to have billboards, Bryant agreed to table the topic until the next meeting. Bryant could not wait to leave the meeting and go to Kingdavid's lunch time concert in the mall one city over. It would take him about an hour to get there and if he left in the next ten minutes, he would make the show on time. Bryant and Chantel missed their chance to go with the group, and although Chantel could not make it, he was happy

IF I BE LIFTED UP   55

to go see his mentee on stage. He had not heard anything about the show, but he knew it had to be good. Kingdavid attracted a crowd when he was out. Kingdavid had grown a great following over the past two months and was doing well for himself, although he was not coming to church. Bryant was eager to speak to him and to see how his ministry of music was going and growing.

CHAPTER Twelve

BRYANT SAT BACKSTAGE. The hustle of the backstage always intrigued him. Dancers and performers moved from place to place swiftly. Light and sound crews ran past at a soft yet lighting fast pace. It always amazed Bryant how the noise and movement behind the scenes never seemed to be heard or thought of by the people sitting in the audience. He thought that must be how blessings work; we can't see God working on our behalf in our backstage. We only see the full production when it takes place. He made a note of those thoughts for a future teaching and continued to watch as the crews prepared for Kingdavid's show.

Bryant took his seat near the curtain as Kingdavid and his dancers went on stage. The ladies began to grind on Kingdavid as he belted out a sexually explicit tune. They rubbed his body as he sang another tune. Kingdavid sang songs about worldly love and lust; these were not the song Bryant was prepared to hear. As the dancers put themselves in sexual positions, Bryant noticed Kingdavid did not sound the same as he did when he sang in church. He still had a wonderful voice, but something was missing from his song. As the dancers began to put themselves in more sexual positions, Bryant decided it was best that he wait for Kingdavid in his dressing room and he left the backstage area.

After Kingdavid finished singing, he hurried to his dressing area to search for Bryant. He felt in his heart he needed to talk to him and he prayed that Bryant had not left. Kingdavid was happy to see Bryant when he arrived in the small dressing area.

"Hey man, I am glad you did not leave. What did you think?" he asked, hoping that he would get honest feedback from his mentor and friend.

"I think we need to talk over lunch, my treat. Now put on some clothes so we can go." Bryant laughed as he walked out to wait for Kingdavid.

They decided to go to a not-so-popular spot so that they could talk and not be interrupted by fans or followers. Once they ordered, Kingdavid asked again about Bryant's thoughts on the show.

"What are you thinking, is my question?" Bryant replied as he sipped his water and waited for Kingdavid to respond.

"Man, I don't know. The company says if I do this stuff and build up a good following, I can pick my songs for my CD and I can sing what I want. I just want to sing. I love the feeling I get on stage, man, not talking about the girls but me singing. Or at least I used to feel that way. Now I don't even sound the same."

Bryant was glad Kingdavid saw that on his own. He did not know how to tell him that he was not the same singer who brought the house down Sunday after Sunday.

"I'm not sure what I am doing anymore, Bryant. Honestly like, all I wanted to do was sing and love the Lord. I know without him I would not even be alive right now, ya know. But the label says no one gets signed these days without some sort of following and because I did not have one this was the best way to guarantee one quickly. So here I am. But I'd trade it all for that feeling again. You know what I mean? That feeling of intimacy with God, that oneness that comes over you when you are in his will. That feeling. Do you think I have gone too far? Do you think I will ever get that feeling again?"

"I am sure you will. God's word says he will never leave us of forsake us. I don't see why not. How are you and Grace?"

"I'm not sure. She came to a show and was very upset. Yeah, you don't have to say it or look that way. I understand why she was upset. She basically gave me a verse to look up and has not had much time for me lately. I don't think she understands how much this could help our future. I mean let's be honest, she is used to the good things in life and I can't provide that if I don't make more money. So in a way this is for the both of us. I am looking out for our future but she does not see that; no one does. I not sure anymore. I want to do it for us, to provide but at the same time it doesn't feel the same. Singing use to be everything now it is just business. But enough about that. How are things going with the church. Sorry I have been out so much."

"Things are going well. I'm thinking of doing a showcase. Lorenz suggested it. I think it would be great to bring some young adult life back to the Christ Love Fellowship before we move into the new church. We will be moving soon and I want to make sure we go out with a bang in the old building."

"You think you got room on the program for me?" Kingdavid asked.

"Sure, man you know we do, as long as you not bringing your dancers and singing that worldly mess." Bryant chuckled.

Both men laughed that as they finished their meal. Bryant knew that he would meet some resistance with the deacons, but he felt that the showcase would be a blessing to many of the members of the church and the community. The showcase would also be a great time at announce the changes in the church. They would not only be moving but new staff would soon be added to the roster of the church. Bryant had interviewed three pastors and their wives for the youth position and in his mind had found the right one. The church was moving in a positive direction although it did not feel as if it was making any progress.

Chapter Thirteen

THE PARKING LOT of Christ Love Fellowship church was pack to beyond capacity. Cars parked on the grass around the parking area and across the street. Everyone came out for the gospel showcase. The energy from inside could be felt in the parking lot. Teens, young adults, and even seasoned saints filed into the church in their dress down attire. When Kingdavid saw Mother Ware in her denim jeans and matching denim vest, he knew it was going to be a praise party like none other. He laughed to himself as he walked up from the overflow parking area. A couple of girls that recognized him from his shows whispered, but he was unconcerned. Tonight was about singing for God. Tonight he would not be singing for money or fame. Tonight, Kingdavid would sing to the glory of God.

He made his way into the church and to Bryant's office. After a brief conversation he and Bryant went into the sanctuary, where Lorenz was playing a worship song. The energy was buzzing as people began to call out to the Lord and wave their hands. The mood was joyful and the spirit of healing swept through the building. Bryant stood at the pulpit for a moment and watched the crowd. He waited for the time to speak, not wanting to speak before being prompted by the Holy Spirit.

The people continued to be engulfed in the spirit, and an energy flowed with ease into the atmosphere. Bryant closed his eyes and absorbed the energy. He received his healing and renewed strength. As the atmosphere calmed, Bryant cleared his throat and opened his eyes.

"Praise God Saints," he began. "Tonight, we will lift up the name of Lord. We will usher in a spirit of worship and praise. Tonight, we will rejoice for this is the day that the Lord has made!" Lorenz began to play the keyboard in the organ setting.

The crowd broke out in a praise dance as the drummer beat life into the drums. After the praise break, artists began the showcase. The first group up was a group of young men from a mime ministry and then a group of dancers. Bryant wished that those ministries were in operation within Christ Love Fellowship. He saw how the people were blessed by the groups and his heart ached for change within the church.

After a couple of groups, Kingdavid stood before the church. He calmly asked that his music be turned off and a hush fell over the crowd. He lifted the microphone and began to sing. Tears began to fall from his eyes as he belted out his love song for the Lord. He sang of sorrow and repentance for leaving the love of his life. A couple of the young ladies looked at Grace, figuring most of the song was about her, but Grace looked at Kingdavid because she knew all of the song was about the Lord. Kingdavid sang until tears fell from his eyes and he kneeled, weeping on the floor.

Bryant walked over to Kingdavid and began praying for him as did Deacon Miller. Once they were done, he got up and the showcase continued with group after group praising the Lord. The showcase was a mixture of all art forms in celebration and worship of Christ. Dancers, rappers, and singers showed their love for the Lord. At the end of the showcase there was a massive altar call where several people accepted Christ or rededicated their lives. The gospel showcase had turned out better than Bryant or Lorenz could have hoped.

    The showcase also caught the attention of one of Bryant's favorite applicants for youth pastor. He was from a church just outside of town and his wife was a trained dance instructor. Bryant felt that the addition of the two of them would bring a more diverse type of ministering to his people. Bryant knew that there was more than one way to minister to God's people and he was determined to be able to offer the believer every possible way to hear from the Lord. The deacons of the church were not impressed with his ideas and would try to block him, however, he felt more than ready after the showcase to handle the deacons. His prayer was that the pastor and his wife would sign on and take over the youth department. Pastor Oaks had taught him the importance of having a strong youth department. He felt that having this pastor over Christ Love Fellowship Youth Department was a winning situation. He was told that his wife would be more than willing to teach dance to the youth as well. That was an added bonus, and Bryant looked forward to interacting with the both of them as co-labors for the Lord. Chantel had met them as well and said she had positive feeling toward them and their membership. She too had been praying for a couple to come into the church and be a blessing to the youth.

Chapter Fourteen

THE CONFERENCE ROOM WAS QUIET. Each member of the meeting sat with pen and agendas waiting for the call to order. The tension was so thick it hovered in the room like a dense fog. Bryant sat at the head of the table in his normal spot. His eyes fixed on the cross that hung across the room. As the last deacons came, in the men prayed and began their meeting. The first order of business was the Gospel Showcase. Several of the deacons argued that it was too worldly, despite the number of people who gave their lives to Christ. They argued that Jesus did not need a hip beat or dance to transform lives. According to this group of deacons there needed to be more reading of the word of God and less singing and dancing. They began to take several scriptures out of context in order to justify their positions. After some time, Bryant stepped in and told the deacons that their position was noted, however the church would still meet believers where they were and explore all the ways of worship.

The new position was the next heated topic of discussion. Pastor Kevin was coming to the church from a nearby city. He had an excellent track record, was young and his wife was trained as dancer which meant the possibility of starting dance at the church.

"Ah, this young lady wouldn't happen to be Corin?" one of the deacons interrupted. "Corin is a former naked lady dancer Pastor; certainly you are not trying to put her in leadership."

"Why not? That was her past, Brother Deacon. Why should we hold that against her? She is married and has a letter of recommendation from her current pastor."

"I just don't think it's right. Not one bit. Not at all."

"Deacons," Bryant began. "Paul murdered Christians, David had a man killed, and some of us have had our own hang ups. Why would we not give this couple a chance?"

"'Cause it ain't right."

"Deacon, you used to gamble all your money away. How can you now sit in judgement of someone who has changed their life just like you changed yours? That is not what Christ Love Fellowship is all about. We don't judge; we love all of God's children just as Christ loves them."

"That right boy, preach that! Love the hell out of them, 'cause they is wicked, but God can fix it. God and only God! Preach it boy, preach." Deacon Miller stood from his seat, shaking his fist and turning his head from side to side with every word he spoke.

"Yes Deacon Miller, we are called to love," Bryant said, holding in his laughter. He enjoyed that passion of Deacon Miller's, and how he was always ready to set the record straight at any given moment about any given subject.

Two of the deacons did not agree with Bryant and decided there would be no love lost if they left. Without warning, they stood, took off their deacon pins, and tossed them in the middle of the large oak table. They were followed by two more before the next order of business was discussed. Deacon Miller offered words of encouragement to Bryant, reminding him that everyone did not make it to the promised land.

Bryant held his head high, although he was very discouraged by the meeting. Once the meeting was over, he quickly headed home. He needed the comfort of his wife more than ever.

Chapter Fifteen

AS SOON AS he walked into the house, she could tell something was not right. She watched Bryant slowly take off his shoes, undo his tie and plop onto the couch. As she walked over to him, she turned on some jazz music with the remote, then sat close to his warm body.

"Are you going to tell me what's wrong?" she asked in a sweet voice. "Whatever it is, we can get through it together. I have your back."

Bryant began to explain the deacons leaving and the drama surrounding the new pastor and his wife. Before he could finish explaining, the phone rang.

"Yes, deacon how are you?" Bryant said, trying to sound cheerful.

"I am fine, young man. Look, I won't hold you long. I just forgot to ask about Sunday's sermon. I know you have your own mind and that's good son, but people wanna hear how they can be blessed by God. You carrying on with all this college level stuff and the people just need to hear how to get what God has for them. If you do that then the people would give more. They know God likes a cheerful giver. Then most of our church problems would be over. You really need to change up your message. Talk about the goodness of the Lord. Maybe have a testimony service where people can come and encourage others to give. Mark my words boy, it will work. That is what cha need to do son, ya hear me?" He finished in his southern drawl.

"Yes, I hear you deacon," was all Bryant could say as he lowered his head and shook it in the palm of his hand. Chantel rubbed his back. She hated to see him in pain and discomfort. She realized that all she could do was pray and that it was not time for the news she had to give him.

"Baby," she said in a soft voice as she rubbed his back. "Can I pray for you?" She took Bryant's hands into hers as they sat on the couch. "Father God," she began softly, "I stand before you Lord, the wife of the man of God who you called to shepherd the flock at Christ Love Fellowship Church. Father you have also called him to be the priest, provider, and protector of my home. Lord you said that he is the head and not the tail. You said he is above only and not beneath. Lord you said no weapon formed against him shall proper. Lord, I am coming to you according to your word. Asking that you restore strength back to his heart. Lord restore his eyes that they might only see you. Restore his heart so that he does you will. Restore the vision that you gave to him. Lord you word says we should pray for our enemies, pray and curse not, so father we come praying for everyone that was and is against the vision that you have called forth. Raise a standard, Lord. We ask these things in Jesus' name, amen." Sweat poured from her face as she regained her composure. Still with her eyes closed, she kept his hand in hers. He could feel the energy running through her hand to his body. She had transcended to another place and was slowly coming back to the couch, the house, on the quiet street.

"Thank you babe, I really needed that. This is harder than I thought it would be. It's like they're coming at me at all angles. I am trying baby, I promise I am trying."

"I know baby and God knows as well. I see you, and if I see

you, we both know He sees you. Babe you just have to do it all unto God. Don't worry about the deacons, the lies, or the rumors."

"Rumors, what rumors?" Bryant said with a look of concern.

"Never mind the rumors, dear. I have it under control," she answered confidently.

Chapter Sixteen

BRYANT AND CHANTEL held hands as they walked into the new church location. The structure was massive. They walked together down the wide foyer area, where they envisioned a future café. For now, it was an open space where they planned to put couches and televisions so that people could watch the service outside of the sanctuary. The dark blue carpet ran from the doors of the church to the doors of the sanctuary. They looked at each other and took a deep breath before opening the doors.

Once they open the doors, they were met with a smaller foyer area, which was an ideal place for the ushers to stand with programs. They were pleased to see that the door did not open directly into the sanctuary. They felt that the sanctuary was a holy place and it needed that extra wall of protection. As they entered the sanctuary, they were greeted by amazingly painted tricolor walls. The shades of blue were heavenly and they matched the chairs that were before them in nice even rows. Chantel let out a big hallelujah as she walked around the spacious area. She spun around several times while Bryant sat on the altar with tears in his eyes. His heart was heavy and full from what God had done. He was so grateful that he lay on the steps of the altar and cried, no longer able to hold in his emotions. Chantel began to praise the Lord even the more when she saw her husband reverencing the Lord. God had brought them both to their promised land.

AS WITH EVERY SUNDAY, Lorenz, Kimmee and Chantel went into Bryant's office to talk before the service. The group laughed at obvious relationship Lorenz and Kimmee were trying to hide. The joked about getting together to not go on a double date, since Bryant and Chantel were the only ones together. The four of them together was just what Bryant needed. Having them come to the office always relaxed him before he taught or preached. He enjoyed the company, although it infuriated the deacons. The deacons felt that the time before church should be quiet and that they should be the only ones to speak to him. Bryant disagreed and did not permit the deacons to see him because they often spent time wanting to talk about his sermons or give him suggestions.

As the clock struck, ten thirty, Lorenz left to start playing his keyboard and Kimmee went to join the praise team. Bryant smiled as he took his wife's hand and led her into the sanctuary. She tugged at her dress, trying to keep her secret intact.

"Are you okay?" Bryant asked, looking over at his wife.

"Yes," she answered quickly, stopping her obsession with her dress.

"You never told me what you had to tell me the other day. What is going on?" Bryant asked in a whisper as they walked through the sanctuary doors.

"We can talk later," she answered as she smiled at the members and took her seat.

Bryant was puzzled by her behavior lately, but decided that God would reveal all in his own time. After the choir sang, Bryant went straight to the word and began preaching about

God's timing. He reminded the members that had they moved the church when they wanted to, they would have missed out on what God had for them in the new location. Although there were many empty seats, Bryant preached as if it were a full house. His voice echoed in the building as he brought forth the words God placed on his heart. The deacons who remained looked at the size of the crowd, then Bryant. They shook their heads in disappointment.

"He is not going to be able to fill this place. I think this was a bad move and I will be right here when it fails to say I told you so," Deacon Jones whispered to Deacon Willis. "This is a shame before God," he continued.

"I know but, you can't tell him nothing. He has that Oaks spirit. Oaks got in his ear before he died and now the boy thinks that he is right, won't take direction. We got to come up with something. Got to get rid of him and his thug life friends." Deacon Willis eyed Kingdavid, who was sitting in the choir stand. "We got to do something, and quick," he finished.

"I am sure we can come up with an idea," Deacon Jones said.

Chapter Seventeen

KINGDAVID SAT on the couch with the love of his life in his arms. Cuddled together, the pair enjoyed a Christian based movie. Grace laid snug in Kingdavid's arms as they watched the movie couple overcome life's challenges with prayer and the power of God. Grace admired the woman in the movie and hoped that if she had those challenges, she would be able to trust God and hold strong to her beliefs as a woman of God. She was happy to be in the arms of her true love. It had been some time since they had time together. Kingdavid had done a number of shows and had a number one selling single. However, he had seemed to return to the Kingdavid she knew and loved after the gospel celebration. She had to admit her heart fell into a thousand pieces when she saw him grinding on other women. After hearing women speak in detail about their fantasies with her man, she had enough and needed time away from the relationship.

Now things were different, or so she hoped. Kingdavid had not mentioned doing shows or a record deal since the Gospel Showcase, which was before the church moved into the new building. He had returned to the choir and their relationship had returned to a steady pace of growth. Grace still wondered about the record deal and if he missed the shows. She was too shy to ask him. She feared that he would say yes or worse, that it would rekindle interest and pursuit into the things of the world. This scared her because at this moment she was in the best place other than the altar: in his arms.

The couple sat quietly, enjoying the movie before being interrupted by the phone ringing. Kingdavid was not going to answer the call; however, the number flashing before him was the record company. He stared at the number before picking up the call. It was as if he was holding his breath for the entire call. When it was over, he let out a long sigh and rubbed his temples.

"What is it?" Graced questioned with worry in her voice.

"The label wants to offer me a deal to create music. They said I can get a signing bonus and start at once. They are giving me three days to decide." He answered with a sad tone. Grace looked puzzled. This was the great news he had been longing for, yet he seemed sad and depressed. "They don't want me to sing Gospel; only R&B." He put his head down.

Grace understood his thoughts. Here he was, faced with the opportunity he had hoped for, but not in the way he wished it would come. Her fears of him leaving to do more shows like the one she saw haunted her as she sat holding her beloved. She was not sure if she could be promised to a secular artist. In her heart she knew that the lifestyle would separate them and she, despite her faith, walked in fear.

Not wanting to talk about it, Kingdavid suggested they finish the movie before it got too late. After the movie he would walk her to her car before going to the church for choir rehearsal.

Instead of going into the rehearsal room, Kingdavid went into the sanctuary. According to the clock he had thirty minutes before rehearsal, which gave him enough time to speak to God about all that was on his mind. The dimly lit room was quiet. Not even the air conditioner could be heard. Kingdavid walked slowly to the altar and laid his body on the steps. He wanted to cry. Fear and pain filled his heart. How could he pass up the chance to make enough money, to take care of his family, marry the girl of his dreams, or give to the church that had given so much to him? How could he let a chance like this slip away? He pleaded with the Lord for answers. Every time he questioned, he heard a still voice say *"What does it profit a man to gain the whole world, and lose his soul?"* Despite this truth, he pleaded again. He understood but wondered about all the ways and people his money could bless. He thought about all the good he could do for the Kingdom with his resources. Yet again, he heard the still voice. *"If I be lifted up, I will draw all men unto me."* Kingdavid sat up, trying to adjust his eyes to the dim light.

"Hey man, you good?" Bryant questioned as he approached.

"Yeah man," Kingdavid answered as he got up on his feet and headed toward Bryant.

"We should grab some wings tomorrow; what do you think?"

"Sounds good," Kingdavid answered as he made his way to choir rehearsal.

CHAPTER *Eighteen*

HER BLACK SHORTS hugged her cream-colored legs tightly. They were long enough to be considered tasteful and short enough to just cover her butt cheeks. Her tightly fitted work tank top said Jack's Wings, and she gossiped with the girl next to her about who sat before them just two table always.

"That is him I tell ya, that is the singer of that song *Make your bed wet*. I promise I would know his fine self anywhere. That is Kingdavid. I don't know who that guy is next to him, but he is hot too! We should go over and take the order; we can work the table together. If it goes well, we can work the two of them tonight." The two girls giggled and headed over to the table where Bryant and Kingdavid sat.

"Hello, I am Gigi and this is Candy. We will be taking your order. If you need anything, just let us know. By the way, are you that hot new singer?" Gigi asked, licking her lips.

"Not sure about hot, but yes I am a singer."

"Well, you tell me what you want, and you can have anything you like." She rubbed her pen over her practically exposed breast.

"We will have the bottomless wings. Oh yes, and two sweet

teas," Bryant interjected as Gigi stared at Kingdavid and Candy stood starstruck.

"Okay, well if you change your mind about my other offer..."

"We won't. Thank you," Bryant interrupted.

The two girls walked off with a disappointed faces as Bryant and Kingdavid chuckled softly.

"Man is it always like that?" Bryant asked. "I couldn't do it. Don't look at me like that. I am for real, man. You got these women forgetting who they are, Lord have mercy. How have you been? What's been up besides skirts?"

"Naw man, you know I ain't down with that. I mean the shows are just that, shows. That's not who I really am, you know that. Yeah, I know you know, but you play too much, B." Kingdavid let out a slight chuckle. "I got to make a choice and it is so hard man. The company wants to give me top dollar, I mean a boat load of money to do this stuff. They're saying I could be the next R. Kelly, without the drama. Bryant, all my life I wanted to be something, to do something big. I want to be able to help Kimmee, my mom, and marry Grace. This would put me there fo sho. But, in my heart I keep hearing voices say what does it profit a man, and if I be lifted up. I am tripping 'cause as bad as I want it, I don't want to disappoint God. I'm bugging right? I mean who does that? Right? Who turns down a deal of a lifetime just 'cause a voice in their head keeps telling them bible verses? I'm so lost. I am not sure what to do, what will be the best way to go. Will Grace and Kimmee support me not doing it, knowing what it would cost? Would you and the church support my decision to do it because I could tithe bigger? I am tripping bad."

Bryant sat for a moment, digesting what he had just heard. He knew that he needed to speak but he wanted to make sure the words he chose were appropriate. He smiled as Candy brought the wings and drinks and waited until she left before he opened his mouth after Kingdavid blessed the food.

"Frist of all, and hear my heart on this, Christ Love does not need your money. Your giving is to the Lord, and just like He can and will rise you up to do something for the church, He can and will raise someone else up if you do not. We are funded by the One that owns the cattle on a thousand hills, not members working. He relies on our obedience, but He does not depend on it. The church will be fine because it is the Lord's. Now as to this money, friend, do not get caught up in the money. That is a trick of the devil. Is what you are doing right and pleasing to God? That's your measuring stick, nothing else. Does it line up with what God said according to His word? That is the bottom line. That's what you really need to know, that and that alone." Bryant took a big bite out of his wing as he and Kingdavid began to eat.

"Thanks man, I know what I need to do then for my family and to become a provider for Grace one day. What about you? How are things really? You got a big church now. I am proud to see the progress. But you look a little down; how is everything with you?" Kingdavid asked, as he bit into another wing.

"Man, things are different, more demanding, and people are changing up on a brother bad. When we had just a couple people show up to church on a Wednesday night it was one thing cause the place was small, but when only a couple show up now in the bigger place it can play on your mind. It is like I have to stay even closer and deeper in the word now, and I thought I was doing pretty good. But it is harder than I thought. No one understands the demands on a pastor. I thought I did but now being in the shoes of Pastor Oaks, I know now why few are chosen. I am not complaining, however, I love what God has done through me. I am learning so much about the Lord and about myself. I am even handling the backstabbing. I never thought I would be able to do that. Don't look so shocked;

everybody has haters, not just worldly people. I think God sometimes gives His saints a double portion. Man those deacons think they are slick. I already know they are plotting something big, but nothing comes to the saints without them being aware. It kills me when church people only think the bible works for them." Bryant chuckled.

"Man, that is what I love about you Bryant. You always keep it real."

"Yeah, well some real work is going to come to help out at the church. I just hope she doesn't start nothing I can't stop before it is too late." Bryant said as they finished their wings. The two of them enjoyed their time together. Bryant knew that next to Lorenz, he could trust Kingdavid. He was an honorable brother who wanted to do the right thing. His honor was why he did not worry about Kingdavid's decision. He knew Kingdavid would be able to take care of his family.

Chapter Nineteen

DEACON JONES SAT on the soft chair waiting to have a word with Bryant. He had been waiting only a couple minutes when he saw her come out of the pastor's office. She was extremely attractive. Her long legs were perfect in her heels. Her outfit was professional, but still sexy, and not one hair was out of place as it framed her beautiful face. She smiled widely at Deacon Jones.

"He will be with you shortly," she said before picking up the phone. "BAE, I mean, Pastor Taylor, there is a gentleman here to see you," she said.

Deacon Jones was taken aback. *Did she just mistakenly call him Babe,* he thought to himself. As he walked past her on his way into the pastor's office, he shook his head. He was sure Deacon Willis would not believe what he was about to tell him. Could it be that the pastor was having trouble in his marriage? His wife, First Lady Chantel, had not been to a couple of services, now that he thought about it. Lately, she had missed bible study and now here Bryant was flirting with the new office worker. This was exactly what they needed to get him to step down.

"Pastor, I am not here to keep you long," Deacon Jones

began. "But, there are concerns about the membership numbers."

"Yes, about those, Honey, I mean Hannah, could you bring me the membership report?" Bryant said as he sat down blushing. He could not believe he made that mistake in front of Deacon Jones as the deacon looked at him crossly.

Hannah strutted into his office confidently and handed him the report.

"Watch who you call honey; would hate for the wife to find out," she whispered loudly as Deacon Jones shook his head in disappointment.

As soon as the men finished their meeting, Deacon Jones was on the phone. During the meeting he wanted to confront Bryant but was unsure of what to say exactly. Would he set out and accuse him of cheating based on his actions? The two of them seemed very close and they had pet names for each other. It was no secret that Mrs. Bryant Taylor had missed several services lately. She seemed to have a cross look during the last service. She stared at the deacons as if she wanted to use some not so Godly words. He was certain that their marriage was in trouble and this new secretary of only a couple of weeks was certainly a hindrance to the couple. If she hindered the couple, that meant that she hindered the church. Bryant could not continue to gallivant with his side piece any longer. The deacons called an emergency meeting as soon as Deacon Jones got into his car.

As usual, they met at Deacon Willis' home. This was their favorite place because it was often empty and they had plenty of room for their egos and big cars. They decided that Bryant should be confronted at the next general body meeting. General body meetings took place every quarter and consisted of all the leaders and any layman who wanted to attend. It was an open forum, similar to a town hall meeting. The deacons felt it would be the perfect place to confront the pastor's dirty deeds in front of everyone. They reasoned that he would not be able to talk himself out of the truth with the entire church present. The normal attendance for the general body was small; however, the deacons felt that once they told their wives all that they had planned the church would be packed. Deacon Miller did not want a part in what he called a witch hunt, however, he had recalled seeing Bryant and Hannah in the same car driving to and from places around town. Hannah was a very pretty girl. The old men admitted if they were not married and rooted in the word of God, they would have tried to date Hannah. One deacon admitted that his thoughts were not to date but to know her in the biblical way of knowing. As in, how Adam knew Eve. Although that made them all laugh, there was a grain of truth in it for all of the deacons. Each of them had to repent for the lust they had in their hearts when they first saw Hannah. Each of them had eyed her perfect size five frame, her long hair, and her oatmeal skin. Each of them had been intoxicated by her scent as she walked by with long legs and high heels. No one questioned who Hannah was after she was introduced as the office manager. She attended another church and only came to Christ Love Fellowship once or twice. All of the deacons agreed that something was going on and it would all be exposed in the general body meeting.

CHAPTER Twenty

CHANTEL DREADED GOING to the general body meeting. She knew that today's meeting was more of a witch hunt than a meeting. She overheard two members speaking in the restroom about the pastor and his wife. Little did they know, she was right there hearing every word. The church gossip was that the pastor was sleeping with his new office manager and that was why his wife had not been to church. In fact, she was leaving him for her old boyfriend who was getting out of jail later that year.

Tears of anger welled up in Chantel's eyes. She wanted to burst out of the stall and begin fighting. She was boiling with rage. However, James 1 came into her mind and she whispered to herself, *"Slow speak, slow to anger."* Once the ladies left the restroom, Chantel came out. Rage had bubbled up and she soon ran back to the stall, vomiting. After cleaning herself up, she joined the others in the large meeting room.

The general body meeting did not take place in the sanctuary. The old members felt that the sanctuary was a place of worship, not where they should talk about business. They mandated that the meetings be held in the education room.

Prior to the church move, members would pack tightly into a small room to talk about the affairs of the church. Now, the church was blessed with a larger area and the education room was the size of the old sanctuary. There was more than enough room for the members, their egos, Robert and his rules of order, and the elephant to sit in the room.

As Chantel entered the room, eyes followed her every move. She confidently walked to the front and sat on the right of her husband as his office manager sat to his left. Traditionally, the deacons opened the meeting with a prayer and a reminder of the rules. Members with questions or comments were to line up at the microphone. Once the question was asked, time was given to the leadership to answer or reply. Members and leaders were placed on a time limit so that the meeting did not last all night. There was nothing left off the table; anything could be asked. The first member to come up was Janis, a single mother with three boys. She quietly walked up to the microphone, secretly wishing someone else would have gone first.

"Um hello," she said shyly. "I was wondering when or if we will get the basketball program back. I have three boys and they loved the program at the old church. I think that is what started them coming to church. Now it is hard to compete with the world for their attention and affection. My boys aren't bad boys by no means, they just need something more to do. I also liked how the men were involved with basketball. The presence of Godly men gave my boys something to look up to. So if possible can we bring that back, thank you," she said as she took her seat and waited for the reply form the leadership panel.

The deacons stared at each other with looks of opposition. The B-Quad as it was called was a ministry that Bryant started. The mission was to use basketball as a way to mentor boys and introduce them to Christ without being pushy. The deacons did not like the group because it attracted boys that had rough pasts. Most of them came from single parent households or were fathers at young ages. They were not the outstanding, business-oriented boys they wanted in the church. They looked at each other, hoping one of them would answer before Pastor Bryant.

"Yes, I understand your concern," Bryant spoke just as one of the deacons was about to say something. "Because I had to take over the church, I was unable to take on the program. I am however praying for someone to take on the challenge of mentoring and reviving the B-Quad. It is something that is dear to my heart. Until then, however, you are welcome to bring the boys up to the church. I am sure the deacons can find work for them to do, or throw the ball around. God did not give us this big church to only have it opened on Sunday and Wednesday nights. We will have opportunities for family and friends to come and fellowship," Bryant finished as the church clapped.

Chantel smiled brightly at her man. She was proud to be Mrs. Bryant Taylor. He was an outstanding man of God. He was obedient to the word of God and a vessel that God used often. She looked over at Hannah and smiled. Hannah smiled at Bryant. She was so glad to call him hers. She had loved him for a long time and now they were finally together. They had spent years apart due to circumstances beyond their control, but they managed to remain close. Now they were finally together. They did not attend the same church, however she always had Bryant's back. That was why she sat next to him, staring daggers at the deacons and other leaders who had caused him so much pain.

A well-dressed man approached the microphone. His suit looked as if it was dripping money, and his cuff links shone under the church lights. He looked like someone they had seen, but no one could be sure. "Hello, my name is Tyrone. I wanted to thank brother Lorenz, and tell the deacons that they should be very ashamed. I came by here one day after having to fill in at work, I was coming to drop off my tithes. I saw some of the deacons and they quickly tried to dismiss me and get me out of the building. I suspect that they thought I was a homeless based on my dirty clothes and face. I reckon that after working all day, I must not have smelled all that fresh either. At any rate, the men I first encountered were so rude and downright mean to me. They told me I could not see the pastor and that I had no business being there. As I walked to my truck, I bumped into brother Lorenz who was kind and asked me if I needed anything. After I told him how I was treated he apologized. He didn't judge me by my looks. That is why pastor, if you would permit me, I would like to build your courts for your B-Quad ministry, and we can even talk about putting a park on that lot we have in the back. What you deacons did not know is that I own the largest construction company in town. I looked messy cause I like to work in the field every now and again, and I don't mind filling in when needed."

"Sir, that would be great. I will have my office manager get your information tonight, and please know this will be addressed in the deacons next meeting." Bryant said this diplomatically, although he wanted to say many ungodly words to the deacon board.

Trying to turn the heat off of the deacons, one of their wives got up after being motioned to by her husband.

"Pastor, before you go blaming and shaming the deacons, let us talk about the real elephant in da room. We talking 'bout you, pastor, why you sleeping wit yo office manager, calling her honey and she calling you BAE. Why your wife ain't been to church, faking like she's sick and you want us to be in church. Now! Talk about that, pastor. What about that? You talking about my husband and them, talk about you." She screamed into the microphone. As the crowd sat, some were amazed, and some dazed.

Bryant took a deep breath and looked at the woman he loved to his right and his honey to the left. He stood slowly and called both women up with him. "I am sorry that some of you think so low of me. I must not be doing a great job as the man of God before you, if you think those things about me. I'll let these ladies that I love dearly speak first. I was going to do this later, but now is the best time considering the outburst. Honey, if you would introduce yourself."

Hannah gave Bryant a long deep hug as some of the members recoiled in their seats. "Hello Christ Love Fellowship." She chuckled at the Love part, wondering where it had gone. "Bryant calls me Honey, and he is the only one who can, by the way. My name is Hannah, and I am Bryant, or Pastor Bryant's, younger sister." The mouths of the deacons and several of the gossiping members fell open. *Sister,* could be heard whispered around the room. Hannah looked at Bryant and noticed a sad look in his eyes. She was very troubled by his expression. The people had no idea how much they had hurt her brother.

"Thank you, Hannah," Chantel said, grabbing the microphone and trying to control her rage. *"Slow to anger,"* she whispered, not want to have to run off to the bathroom because she was sick again. "I have not ever faked a thing in my life. I don't do fake. I don't do fake hair, nails, or fake money. I dang sure don't do fake friends. Some of y'all can miss me with that *hello, how are you* after today. Now to address my being sick, I have been trying to tell my husband, but he has been occupied with the church and I knew it could wait. I wanted it to be special, but I guess we will all find out together since y'all are nosy," she caught herself. "Since y'all are so concerned. I happen to be pregnant!" She shouted into the microphone. Bryant looked shocked, then grabbed her and kissed deeply. Members of the church gasped while others clapped. Hannah hugged her brother and sister in law.

"Brothers and sisters, if you don't mind, I'd like to end this general body meeting. I hope to see you all Sunday for church," Bryant said with a smile as he held his wife close.

CHAPTER
Twenty-one

BRYANT SAT in the empty parking lot of the park. His car faced the river. He watched in silence as the rain danced on the river. He sighed as the wind blew away everything but the cares on his heart. Bryant's eyes filled with tears. He inhaled slowly. His heart weight a ton. He continued to watch the river water flow past. The faint sound of Anthony Evan's worship music played in the background. He rested his head against the driver's seat. He was filled with sorrow. The rain mocked his tears as it began to stream heavily from the sky. He found it hard to catch his breath as he sobbed. His mind filled with ungodly thoughts as he moaned.

"End it now," a dark voice in his mind said, "end it all now." The dark voice continued, "You can end it now. They don't respect you at that church. How could they think that you would cheat on your wife? I know, you don't have the image of a real man of God. They think you are a joke. End it now, just drive off the pier into the river below. They are not going to miss you. Chantel is strong; she can raise the baby. That's if the baby even lives. You know she had that abortion. The baby might not make it. End it now. It's just not worth it. Why are you doing all this anyway? Look at Kingdavid; he wants to do good but he is taking a major pay cut. What kind of God wants you be broke? I tell you, the only peace is in death Bryant, end this now. It won't even hurt. You will be out of all this pain in your heart. You got deacons plotting on you, if you can't trust church folk... Bryant, end this now."

Bryant rolled down the window and allowed the rain to come into the car. The cold rain fell against his face and mixed with his tears. He rested his head on the door as the rain poured in the car window. His face and shirt became soaked. He took a deep breath and wailed in pain. His screams went unheard. No one was around for blocks. In his car, he and the dark voice sat together.

"Why are you here, really? Why? You have no purpose. Your ministry is broke, your bills are high, and you have no way out. Bryant, just give it up and end this pitiful life now. Do it, DO IT!" The dark voice said. Bryant sobbed even more as the rain swept his tears away.

Was the voice right? Bryant, despite his foundation, was not doing as well as he wanted. He had grown up in the ministry. He was a pastor's son, grandson, and great grandson. He was preaching before he could walk, according to his mother. He was called at an early age and despite the traditional couple of years of running from the call, he was devoted to the ministry. If Christ Love Fellowship Church was truly the place for him, why would God allow ordained men to speak against him? Bryant was perplexed. Was he truly the one God wanted to use? "NO!" the dark voiced shouted in his soul, then whispered, *"end it."*

Bryant sat up. He was sure the dark voice was telling him the truth. It was better if he was not alive. The church surely did not want him. He was so consumed with other things that his wife did not even tell him she was expecting. She could just get rid of it, she had done it before. Bryant stepped out of his car and began to walk on the pier. The rain fell gently as he looked at the water below. The water was just deep enough to do as the dark voice suggested. The loud shrill of a bird overhead caused Bryant to look up. As he held his head up, he saw a rainbow in the sky. *"God's promise,"* he whispered.

Like a wave, the promises of God flooded Bryant's head. The force was so strong that he grabbed his head with both hands. As if he was hit by a mighty wind, his body rocked back and forth. Promise after promise caused him to fall to his knees. Weeping, he began to repent and to worship. "No weapon!" he declared, "formed against me shall prosper. Though I walk through the valley of the shadow of death, I shall fear no evil."

Promise filled his mind and he begin to worship on the pier as the rain came to a peaceful stop. The pier that overlooked the river was no longer a pier. The pier was an altar, and the park had become a sanctuary. After his worship, he slowly stood to his feet and walked to the car. As he turned on the car, Tye Tribett began to sing about taking it all back. Bryant's spirit shook in agreement. Bryant could hear the spirit say, *"If I be lifted up from the earth, I will draw all men unto me."* For Bryant, that meant it was not about a prosperity message or commercials. It was about proclaiming and lifting Christ above all. Showing people how to lift up Christ and live Christ. Bryant pulled onto the highway determined to lift Christ above the Earth.

CHAPTER Twenty-two

BRYANT SAT in his office with new vitality. It had been three weeks since his altar experience. Chantel was feeling better and although she could not, he could see her tummy starting to round slightly. Three more of the deacons decided to worship elsewhere, and he had hired a new youth pastor. Pastor Kevin was ready to get started at once and the church had growth on its horizon. Bryant was determined to do what the Lord said and nothing else. He was no longer following traditions and the old way of doing things. In several sermons since his encounter in the rain, he preached about not doing things as they had been done. He proclaimed that Christ Love Fellowship Church would do things according to the word of God, not the word of man or deacon.

As he worked on his next sermon, there was a light knock at the door. When he looked up, he was surprised and pleased to see Kingdavid at his door. Kingdavid was dressed in modest apparel and was not the same half-necked gentleman Bryant had seen months before. This Kingdavid was a man of God and the word was apparent by the way he stood in the doorway and how he carried himself.

"Pastor Bryant, do you have a second? I would like to have a word with you," Kingdavid said as he walked into the door.

"King sure, what can I do for you sir?" Bryant said with a smile.

"I was hoping to talk about the B-Quad." Kingdavid sat in the plush chair across from Bryant. "You know the B-Quad is close to my heart. If it had not been for the quad, I would not be the man I am today. Something as simple as playing ball on Saturday changed my view about being a man and about God. I know that there are other brothers out there who need that experience. They need to see men of God just living life so that they can live a Godly life. They need us Bryant, to show them Christ-led men, the church, the fullness of God, and His true representatives. I know that you are busy with the church and I respect that, so if you do not mind I would like to head up the B-Quad. I believe that the simple act of playing basketball can shape and change a young man. Nope, scratch that, I know that playing ball on Saturday would help change a young man. I know this because it did for me. I want to be a blessing for others," Kingdavid stated sincerely.

Bryant sat back in his chair and eyed Kingdavid. He had come so far from where he started. Bryant remembered the slang talking thug who fought with his son's mother on the basketball court. Now here he sat, a man after God's heart. A young man wanting to disciple others and lead them to Christ as he had been led. A smile came upon Bryant's face at the thought of the wonderful things Kingdavid was going to do for the kingdom of God.

"Kingdavid, I think that is a wonderful idea. Can you start this Saturday coming?" Bryant hoped he would say yes. The basketball courts had just been completed and he did not want them to go unused for a long period of time.

Kingdavid was more than willing and nodded yes as he grinned from ear to ear.

Friday night, Kingdavid prayed fervently that someone would show up for the first B-Quad ball game. He would feel horrible if no one was there. He knew in his heart that God wanted him to revive the ministry and that it was a great way to bring men to Christ. All night, he prayed and tossed and turned. Saturday morning found him up and ready before dawn as if it was Christmas morning, and he was a seven year old. He quickly showered and ate breakfast before heading to the court.

The game was supposed to start at ten according to the flyers that he put all over the community. It was now ten thirty and no one showed up for the event. Kingdavid stood alone on the basketball court bouncing his ball. He was about to give up when his watch struck eleven and he was alone. As he walked to the park bench, a young man showed up on the court.

"Eh, is dis dat church basketball game?" A thin, mocha complected man said.

"Yes, this is that church basketball game," Kingdavid translated. "You want to play?" he asked.

"Yeah, I'll play you," the man said.

The two of them played one-on-one for an hour. After the game, Kingdavid handed the man a bottle of water from his cooler.

"Man you got some skills; what is your name?" Kingdavid asked.

"They call me Mike, short for Michael."

"Well Mike, I am Kingdavid. We play every Saturday, so you are welcome to come back." Kingdavid looked around, "And feel free to bring some friends." He chuckled.

"Wait, that's it? You not gonna try to church me? You no, tell me bout da Lord and what not?" Mike questioned.

"I can tell you if you want to know, but this is just a game amongst peers. We just hanging out. You look puzzled; let me see if I can explain it this way. I love the Lord, and yes, I am a

Christian, but I live this thing daily. It's not about being up in the front of the church on Sunday. It is not a Sunday morning, Wednesday night kind of life. I die daily to the things of this world. This my lifestyle. The way I live my life. So no there isn't anything else. I like ball and wanted to get with some men to play. I like hip hop, so sometimes we have music playing, Trip Lee, KB, Andy and so on, and I love the Lord so I do it all to his glory. Ya get it?" Kingdavid waited on a reply.

"Yea man, I feel ya. Who were those artists you named? K something, Andy, and Trip, I believe you said?" Mike questioned.

"Oh, they are some of the best MC's in the game. I will play some of their music next week. Will you be here?"

"Yeah, what time?"

"Ten," Kingdavid said. The men shook hands and went their separate ways.

The next Saturday, as he had promised, Mike showed up to play. Kingdavid brought his CD player and they listened to Christian Hip Hop while they played ball. Mike began to ask questions about the lyrics and some of the messages in the content. Mike attended basketball every Saturday for a month, and each Saturday, he became closer to Kingdavid and closer to the things of the Lord.

"How is B-Quad coming along?" Bryant asked one afternoon.

"Man, I just got one dude," Kingdavid said in disappointment.

"Do not despise small beginnings, my brother. Jesus left a flock to get one. One is a strong number because one can put a thousand to flight. Be encouraged, brother. God has got it in his hands," Bryant said as they walked to their cars.

Mike and Kingdavid played for another month, and Kingdavid saw Mike grow into the faith. Just as Kingdavid was about to give up, he noticed a group of men walking toward him with Mike. Mike walked up and introduced Kingdavid to the crowd. Mike was very nervous because he had never done his sort of thing. Once everyone was selected, the group of men played a round of basketball.

Mike continued to come to the basketball games, each time bringing more and more friends. Kingdavid knew the ministry was a success when three of the ballplayers came to the church and two of them, one being Mike, joined the church. Kingdavid found his purpose.

CHAPTER Twenty-three

BRYANT SAT in his office for a moment after his friend and wife left. He silently prayed that today's sermon would be well-received by this congregation. This was his out-of-the-box moment. He waited this long because he wanted to have a plan started before he exposed the vision to everyone. Now that the B-Quad, the youth department, the dance ministry and choir were up and running, he felt this was the perfect time.

Kingdavid was doing an excellent job with the B-Quad. At first Bryant had to offer council because the turnout was low. Just as Bryant said, the numbers grew, and now about twenty five men were showing up each Saturday to play ball and fellowship. More of the men stayed to help the deacons around the church after the game, and some came for Sunday services. Bryant was very proud of the man and leader Kingdavid was becoming.

Bryant was equally excited about the Youth Department. Pastor Kevin was a wonderful addition to his staff. He was already planning youth events with the first one being a locked in to take place in two weeks. Corin, Kevin's wife, was a helping hand to the youth and a dance instructor. She had taken a group of talented girls and introduced them to the power of the anointing. Bryant saw the practice for Youth Sunday and was very impressed with the level of worship that came from young willing vessels.

Bryant smiled as he looked at a picture of Lorenz and Kimmee on his display case. The two of them had been dating for some time and after seeing them work together in the church with the choir, Bryant knew that they would marry soon. The two of them had a chemistry that was ordained. Together, they turned a wannabe Florida Mass Choir into a great choir all on its own.

Bryant knew that now was the time to share the new vision for Christ Love Fellowship Church as it was given to him by God one day while sitting by the river in the rain. He knew everyone would not accept his teaching. He knew that above all, he had to be obedient to God. As he stared at the pictures on his wall, he was determined in his spirit to do what the Lord God required for him to do. He stood, adjusted his suit and headed to the sanctuary. Waiting for him at the door was his wife. He smiled at the sight of her growing frame and grabbed her hand, kissing it gently before they walked into the sanctuary.

"Giving honor to God." Bryant began his sermon in the same way he always did, but this sermon was unlike the teaching before. Bryant began to tell the congregation that today was a new day, and that new advancements for the kingdom needed to and would be made. Some members clapped and said amen while others waited to see what he meant by change. They were not pleased.

The congregation of Christ Love Fellowship was made up of traditional church members who had been in the same church most of their adult life, and young adults who were on fire for the work of the Lord. This mixed crowd was a slight problem because the only thing they agreed on was that they loved Christ. Bryant told the group that Christ Love Fellowship was only concerned with lifting up the Lord above the Earth for all of the world to see. He forbade the commercializing of Christ. He told his members that they were commanded by God to lift up Christ which meant to live Christ 24/7 and 365. Bryant told his church that they were going to be the church for others and live the church for the world to see. They were going to lift up Christ by being Christ to the world. He asked them to watch what they listen to, watch and entertain themselves with, and to avoid compromising their vessels. Bryant proclaimed that he was a willing vessel for the Lord and that his family would live Christ. Then he asked if anyone would join his family in lifting up Christ and the entire church erupted in praise.

Members began to shout with loud voices and rejoice in the Lord. Mother Ware ran up and down the aisle with a vagarious step. Lorenz played life into the keyboard. At the sound of his playing, Deacon Willis began to leap where he stood. The spirit was so high that the teenagers who normally passed notes stood and waved their hands as tears of surrender streamed down their faces. Chantel sat with her arms stretched out, bent over, shouting and blessing the name of the Lord. The presence of the Lord could be felt throughout the church. Everyone in the building was caught up in the Holy Ghost. Never before had mass praise broke out in the church at that level. It was unseen yet it was happening throughout the church that Sunday.

Unable to speak, Bryant sat back down and watched the spirit move throughout the church. Once the mood calmed, the secretary came up to do church announcements. She reminded the parents and youth that they would be going on their college tour trip the next Saturday. They would visit three colleges in one day and needed to be on time.

Shouts of amen rang through the church again, this time by the youth members. The youth had taken a liking to Pastor

Kevin and his wife Corin. They enjoyed the program he outlined, and parents were pleased with his leadership. He and his wife modeled a Godly marriage for many of the children in single-parent homes. Parents were grateful to have a teenage-free weekend and blessed the Lord as well.

CHAPTER Twenty-four

SATURDAY'S YOUTH trip was on its way and on time. The youth ages fourteen to seventeen arrived at the church at eight in the morning. Bryant was there to greet them and to give them a pep talk before they boarded the bus sponsored by the young adult ministry. He and Lorenz had plans to shop for music equipment, however after seeing the number of youth attending the trip, they decided they should attend to help keep an eye on the teenagers. They figured the enemy could do a work with young teens on a college campus.

The bus ride to the state college was short, just a couple miles from the church. Many of the teens felt that it was too close to home. They walked past the state-of-the-art dorms without a care. They paid little attention to the award-winning programs or the amazing campus landscape. Some of the youth did find the fact that this school offered scholarships for just about everything interesting. When asked if they wanted website information to apply, most of them said they did not need information. This came as a shock to adults in the group. They thought that most of the youth would want information based on their facial expressions as they toured the campus. Many of them looked like they had stepped into Oz or Wonderland. Yet, no member of the tour wanted information. This perplexed the adults because the purpose of the tours was getting them information.

As they entered the bus, Kevin could not contain his curiosity. "Hey guys, I got a question. Why did no one want any information?"

"With all respect, Pastor," one of the boys said, "no one wants to go to school at home."

"Yeah," the group said.

"How you gonna party at home? My mama would be expecting me to be in church every Sunday and stuff. College is about being free to be how you are. You can't be free and in bondage at the same time. Ain't that right, Pastor Bryant? You can't be bound and free, you taught that," one of the young girls said.

Bryant was pleased that they had some of the message. Everyone assumed that they were just on devices playing games and texting. He needed to use this moment as a teaching point, to ensure that they understood the faith.

"IT'S great that you listen to the teaching. You know how you all say you don't like fake people that act one way with you and then another way with other friends?" The entire group responded with a yeah. "Well how real are you, if you are in church on Sunday and singing Jesus in the choir, but you are scared to go to school near home cause you do not want to get caught in your mess? Now I am not saying you cannot have fun, but I am saying that fun should not disconnect you from Christ. If your Jesus wouldn't do it, why would you?" Bryant could see that his words had some of the youth thinking. It was the Pastoral team's prayer that they would not raise another generation of lukewarm Christians who only served and believed on Sunday. The goal was to be a body of believers that lived Christ.

Bryant could see that making Christ a lifestyle was not going to be an easy task. As the bus pulled into the next stop, the youth began to question why they were there. It was after all, a community college. They looked shocked as they stepped off the bus. The team had to explain to them the benefits of doing a two-year school first, and that many of them would be blessed by taking this route. Many of them questioned the steps as if it meant they would be inferior.

"Y'all need to know the first shall be last and the last first," Lorenz said as they walked through the halls of the college.

"Hey, that's in the Bible," one of the boys said, making the others laugh at his *Aha* moment. "What? It is!" He shouted to the laughing group of youth.

As the tour went on, the youth seemed to gain a fresh perspective and new understanding about their future. After the community college, they headed out of town to a school that was a two-hour drive away. Luckily for them, they were able to catch the late tour and attend a campus ministry event.

After the tour, the youth were excited about the University and the campus ministry mixer. They were interested in how Christian kids had fun in school. The Saturday night event was filled with games, food, and music. It was a great time had by all. Bryant was pleased that they had the opportunity to see young people living Christ while in college. He thanked Kevin over and over on the bus ride back to the church for providing the opportunity for the youth. Kevin, being a humble man, gave all the glory to God. He told Bryant that he had not seen anything yet. Youth Sunday was the fourth Sunday, and approaching quickly. The youth department was working hard to make sure that youth Sunday was a blessing to others just as every other Sunday was a blessing to many people.

CHAPTER Twenty-five

BRYANT WALKED into the church at what he would have thought was early Saturday morning. After all, it was ten in the morning and most people would have just begun their commutes for the day. The members of Christ Love Fellowship, however, called this Saturday Super Saturday and everyone was at the church for one reason or another.

Super Saturdays were the last Saturday before the youth Sunday. It was a time when everyone practiced. The junior ushers had practice and a meeting, the choir had rehearsal, and the drama and dance groups also practiced. The fact that all the youth met made it easy for parents to get together. In addition to the youth practices, the church was filled with mission meetings and helps department meetings and programs. Bryant walked in the church amazed at what God had done in such a short period of time. He was moved to tears as he saw saints living Christ inside the church and bringing people from outside the church in to help and work.

As he wiped his eyes, he went to his office to prepare the youth Sunday service. Bryant was experiencing some trouble with his sermon. He knew his content and his subject, but he struggled to put it in words. He plan was to come from Jeremiah 29:11, and although it was a passage he knew well he could not put it together. Putting his pen down in frustration, he began to pray for direction.

Bryant could feel eyes looking at him as he finished his prayer. He opened his eyes. Standing before him was a five-foot-nine, skinny, dark cocoa-complexioned Rashad. Rashad, now seventeen, did not get into as much trouble as he did in his did in his early teen years. He was convicted of vandalism for tagging walls downtown with a group of friends, shoplifting, and possession of a weapon. He was a minor at the time and was able to get off with prayers and community service. For the past two years, Rashad had escaped trouble and was turning out to be a good student. The reformed Rashad stood before Bryant in his office doorway with a slight smile.

"Come in son, what can I do for you?" Bryant asked. Nervously, Rashad walked in the office and sat down.

"Sir, I was wondering if I could talk to you about Sunday. I know it's youth Sunday and I think it's a great time to do this." Rashad took a deep breath. "I want to bring the word Sunday. Now before you say no, please hear me out. I know I haven't always been the best young man, but God has done something to my heart. I know that I have made mistakes and bad choices, but God has a purpose for everything we go through, and I really feel like I should do this Pastor. I even have a text that I will be coming from."

"Really, which text?" Bryant asked, enjoying the passion of the young man.

"God has instructed me to speak on Jeramiah 29:11. What do you think about that?"

Bryant smiled.

"I think that God is amazing, and I think that you will be amazing as well. I would love for you to address the youth."

After a brief conversation about church protocol, Rashad left to continue his studying for the message he would bring on

Sunday. Bryant was happy that the Lord's message was coming out of the mouth of a youth on Sunday. He felt that the youth would receive being taught by one of their own.

As Bryant watched the anointed young man walk out of the door, he could not stop himself from smiling. God had answered his prayers. The word that was in his heart was going out, and his members were living Christ. The youth were showing him that God had prepared a future for the church. Bryant's life and ministry seem to be coming together. As he left the church for the day, he could see the mass choir assembling. He was amazed at the size and age range of the choir. So many people young and old would gather to sing one song at the end of the service. Mother Ware greeted him as he walked out, and she walked in the door.

As she walked into the rehearsal space, she was pleased to see so many faces, young and old. She noticed a couple of new faces, gentlemen she had only seen in the area. She saw one older gentleman and what appeared to be his grandson. She heard the young man say grandpa in conversation. She could not help but stare at the older gentleman. His closely shaved gray beard and mustache combination had her intrigued as she eyed his clear mahogany complexion. She could tell by his build that he was an active man. She sashed by him hoping to catch his eye. She smiled shyly and found her seat in the alto section.

"Lorenz, who is the new bass?" she asked, trying to act as if she was not flirting from across the room.

"That is Mr. Sims, and that is his grandson in the tenor section. They just moved here from Ohio, and no, there is not a Mrs. Sims," Lorenz answered.

This made Mother Ware giggle like a schoolgirl. She was over being Mrs. Ware a year after her beloved Herbert passed. Being a woman of God, she was waiting on the Lord. She looked over at him again and to her pleasure, he was noticing her as well. She silently thanked God as Lorenz started the choir practice.

Once on one accord, the choir sounded wonderful. They were prepared to break chains and set captives free. Lorenz looked over at Kimmee smiled. He was blessed to have her in his life and in his ministry. He thought for a moment about life without her and frowned. Not liking the way it made him feel, Lorenz knew what needed to be done.

CHAPTER
Twenty-six

CHANTEL PULLED up to the church amazed by the turn out. Cars were parked in every spot but her own. Luckily, she had a reserved spot close to the business office. Gone were her days of looking for a spot and making the walk to the church. This was helpful due to the fact that her energy level was no longer the same. The little blessing that grew inside of her was zapping her of her vibrance. Despite her lack of gusto, Chantel was happy to be having Bryant's daughter. She knew that she would be treated like a princess because Bryant always treated her like queen.

As she walked into the church, she could hear the young intercessors praying. It was the church's custom to allow the youth to run the whole service. She smiled at the young greeters as she entered the church and walked past the young men in suits providing security. She went to Bryant's office. When she opened the door, she smiled as Bryant sat across from the nervous Rashad who was bringing the word of God.

She admired the sharply dressed Rashad. Rashad wore a dark gray suit with a light gray shirt, a yellow, white, and gray tie and gray shoes. She remembered the young intercessor having on a yellow dress and the greeters and gentlemen in the same color. She wondered if the children plotted to do this. It looked very nice and was something she would have to talk to Bryant about doing on Sundays. *The Bible did say that a child would lead them,* she thought to herself. She could not wait for her child to be a part of the youth at Christ Love Fellowship Church.

Once Bryant finished with the young man, he left him to pray and joined his wife in the sanctuary. The children led the church into outstanding worship. The choir sang of God's love and faithfulness. The message was well-received by the body of believers. They stood and waved their hands as they sang and worshiped. They shouted praises to the Lord and danced as David danced. The dance ministry continued the celebration of the goodness of God with their dance. The atmosphere was set for the word of God as Rashad got up to speak.

After exchanging the normal church greetings he cleared this throat and began to speak. "Saints, the Bible says I know the plans I have for you, and that these plans are for our good. Plans of God equal our good in the end. Another word says that all things work for the good of them. Plans equal good. Turn to your neighbor and say, plans equal good." The church did as he said as some smiled with joy over his words. "Now I'm going to mess you up ,'cause I was like, God if it all works for my good, why do I experience bad things even when I am doing right.? That is when I heard Him say, *'Plans equal good.'* Here is what I mean.

God has a plan, and that plan is for our good in the end. So even if it is not right now, it will be made right in the end. In the end it has to work, and God already know this; He says it. So yes, I may be in a struggle right now, but His promise is that He knows what He is doing and it will work. It will prosper me, it will be for my good. It may not look that way now, but if I focus on Christ, it will be."

The church erupted in praise at the sound of the young

man's word. Rashad had made his family proud. He also made Bryant proud, but most importantly, he pleased the Lord. As Rashad sat down, full of the anointing, the mass choir came up to sing. Members of all ages came together to sing on one accord. They sang the selections before altar call and marked the transition from one group in charge to the next. Once their song was done, the adults would take over the service and positions within the church. During the altar call, ten people joined the church.

Bryant and his friends sat in his office talking about the wonderful service that they just witnessed. It had been some time since they all got together, and they missed each other and their fellowship. Kimmee suggested that they get together and do a triple date. The group chuckled at the sound of a triple, but agreed that was what they needed.

CHAPTER Twenty-seven

BRYANT and the pleasantly plump Chantel met Lorenz, Kimmee, Kingdavid, and Grace at the movie theater. It had rained earlier that day, and puddles covered the street. Bryant playfully offered to carry Chantel, who swore she as too heavy, but decided to hold her hand instead. As they approached the group, Grace was relieved that she was not the only one in jeans. Chantel wore a pair of dark washed jeans and a tunic. Grace wore the same style of jeans with a t shirt. Kimmee was the only one who wore a dress. Her dress was date-night appropriate, and it fell effortlessly over her curves. This was Kimmee and Lorenz's regular date night and she enjoyed dressing up. Kimmee had been dating Lorenz for a couple of months, not long enough in her mind to show up anywhere looking average. Lorenz being an unofficial style guru appreciated the time Kimmee took to make herself runway perfect. He appreciated so much about who she was as a woman.

The group laughed from the opening scene until the end of the movie. Each couple, wrapped up in each other, sat enjoying every comedic joke that was thrown at them. They stumbled out of the movie, laughing and repeating jokes, acting out scenes, and remembering each line. The group decided to walk to a nearby restaurant that was on the other side of the movie complex. The rain was completely gone and most of the puddles had dried up.

Once in the restaurant, the group sat at a table in a private room with the band playing. The group was not only able to eat, they were also able to dance. Kingdavid whispered in Grace's ear and the couple hit the dance floor pulling each other close.

"Look at them, so young and in love. You think they will get married?" Chantel questioned.

"I know he loves her, and he wants to. I am not sure when. You know my brother is a proud man. He wants to make sure he can provide for her like she is used to living. I have spoken to her and she is not like that at all. She doesn't want half of what he is trying to provide. She would be happy living above the garage if that meant being with Kingdavid. She could care less about her daddy's money."

"Sounds like she knows money can't buy love," Lorenz said.

"No, it cannot. So sad that people get caught up in what someone has. Lucky for my brother, she is not like that. I am sure he will marry her."

"Mrs. Taylor, will you dance with me?" Bryant asked, standing up and taking his wife's hand. She willingly followed him to the dance floor. They danced slowly as the band played softly.

"What do you think we should name the baby?" she asked, holding her husband close.

"I want to name her Faith, if that's okay with you. Faith, because great is His faithfulness."

"That is so beautiful. Faith it is." Chantel giggled as the baby inside leaped.

. . .

THE COUPLES ENJOYED their wonderful meal and were ready for dessert. They had laughed, danced, and eaten to their hearts' content.

"This is nice," Lorenz began, "we got a married couple, a dating couple, and an engaged couple. We should be a TV show." Everyone at the table looked confused as a waiter came over, giving Kimmee a plate with a cupcake topped with a wedding ring, and *will you marry me* written in cream on the edge of the plate. Kimmee covered her face to hide her surprise. She had turned red.

"Well," the group said. She nodded her head yes before kissing Lorenz for the first time.

CHAPTER
Twenty-eight

BRYANT SAT IN HIS OFFICE. Unlike a normal Sunday where Bryant sat with friends, Bryant sat alone. He took a deep breath and looked over his spacious office. He had come from a little closet-sized office in a small store front to his new office in a mega church. He looked at his shelf of pictures. He smiled at the sight of Pastor Oaks. His eyes began to tear. His pastor had been gone for a little over a year and he missed him. He missed being able to ask questions about leadership. He chucked to himself. He could have used his help dealing with the deacons when he first started. On his dying bed, Pastor Oaks advised Bryant to lift up Christ and to lead and live as Christ would live. This advice had carried Bryant for the entire first year as the pastor of Christ Love Fellowship Church.

Over this year, Bryant learned a lot about people. He could have used help dealing with his deacon board, men who tried to hang him spiritually and kill him emotionally. Bryant was able to overcome his adversity with prayer and dedication to the Lord. Some of the deacons had left the church, but some was not all. Some was only a few. Bryant had a thriving deacon board. Deacon Willis was more on board and was a willing active member of the church.

Thinking of Deacon Willis, Bryant stared at a picture of Kingdavid. He was so proud of the man that Kingdavid had become in a short year. He had gone from thug life to Christ life. Bryant remembered seeing Kingdavid on stage and speaking to him when he decided to completely change his life. Kingdavid was now the leader over the B-Quad ministry and witnessing to others. Kingdavid was lifting Christ up, and Bryant was amazed at what God had done in the life of the young man. Bryant gathered his thoughts and things and headed to the sanctuary for his Pastor's Anniversary Celebration.

The church was decorated with poster size pictures of ministries working within and outside of the church. There were pictures of men playing basketball and praying together. Pictures of the youth outings, choir and dance. Pictures of the meals for members being delivered. Pictures of all the ministries at work. On the overhead screen, the words LIFT UP CHRIST. LIVE A CHRIST LIFE were bold. Bryant was moved to tears as he had never thought he would have made it this far. He stood by his wife and touched her stomach.

Chantel had only a couple weeks left before she would give birth to their daughter, Faith. She was anxious to meet the little blessing who had been growing inside of her and kicking her at night. She was sure that her little girl was going to be a daddy's girl and a tomboy. She did not mind at all as long as the two loves of her life were there. For Bryant, his life had come full circle in a year, and he was certain that God would bless his family, church and friends if they continued to lift up Christ.

CHAPTER Twenty-nine

Two Years Later

"MAN HOLD STILL," Bryant said to the nervous Lorenz as he helped him with his suit. "Why are you so nervous?"

"Man, I don't know. I hate these things, you know that."

"Come on gentlemen, it is going to be a glorious day," Kingdavid interrupted.

Just as the men prepared to walk down the aisle to marry off their friend, Deacon Willis came in the door.

"I know it's almost time, but I wanted to say sorry. I judged you and that was not living Christ. I wanted you to know that I think you are a fine young man." Just as quickly as he came in, he was gone, leaving Bryant, Lorenz and Kingdavid staring at each other. The men went to take their places at the front of the church. Soft music played as the women they loved began to walk down the aisles.

Chantel came down the in her light blue maid of honor dress looking as beautiful as she did the first time Bryant saw her. Bryant walked down memory lane as she came closer. Following Chantel was Kimmee, and Lorenz was beaming bright as a Christmas tree. Anyone in the room cold see the love he had for Kimmee in his eyes. They sparkled and danced as he looked at her. They were married now for one year, although Lorenz would often say it felt like yesterday was when they said I do. Toddling behind Kimmee was a two year old Faith. Faith threw a fist full of flowers every couple of steps as if she was tossing softballs.

Walking on those scattered flowers was Grace. She walked with her father, who had no problem allowing her to marry her king. Her father had seen something in Kingdavid over the years, and although he could not put his finger on it, Kingdavid knew.

"What did you do to my father to get him to like you?" Grace asked as they danced at the reception.

"Just what the pastor said. I didn't worry about it. I just lived a Christ life and lifted up Christ."

The two of them kissed.

AFTERWORD

I hope that you have found this story to be entertaining and edifying. If you have ever wondered if you are loved, let me tell you: You are loved and created by the BEST. God loves you so much that he sent His son to die for you (and me) so that you (and me) could live in eternity with Him.

If you have not accepted Jesus as your personal savior, I would like to extend you an invitation. Say this with me: *Father, I believe that you have sent your son Jesus into the earth for me. I believe that you have a plan for my life, and I want to invite you into my life as my personal Lord and Savior. Amen.*

Yeah, Sis/Bro, the Bible says that you will be saved if you believe in your heart and confess with your mouth. I suggest you get a Bible and start reading God's love letter and Life Manual. You can get a physical Bible or download the YouVersion application. I like the digital Bible because you can read across the different translations and have free devotionals. I am loving the devotional feature. You can also study alone or with friends.

Next, you should find a church. A church will provide you with a family to walk alongside you in your journey. Please know that no person is perfect; therefore, no church will be perfect. Sis/Bro don't look for perfect; look for God's love.

ACKNOWLEDGMENTS

I still cannot get over the fact that right know you are reading my book. Look at God, won't He do it! I hope that you found this story as enjoyable as I did writing it. While it is time to put Lorenz, Chantel, Bryant, Grace, Kimmee, and Kingdavid away, I have a whole list of other characters I hope you will fall in love with soon.

I would like to start my thank you list with God. I pray that these words add a blessing to the lives of readers. I would then like to thank my readers for taking the time to read If I be Lifted Up. I pray that you have been entertained and inspired, drawn in, but not drawn away from our wonderful faith. To my wonderful hubby and family, thank you for allowing me to be an author. To my AIP family and Mrs. Denora Boone, to say thank you would not be enough. I LOVE YOU.

As we depart for a short while, I look forward to seeing you in the next story.

Read and Be Blessed,
She Nell

OTHER BOOKS BY SHE NELL
A GOOD THING

A Good Thing 2: If I be Lifted Up

A Good Thing 3: Vengeance is Mine

Blacklove Magic: Love in the Streets Heaven in the Sheets

Joyful Noise: The Hot Mess Choir

The Devil Thought He Had Me

Her Pleasures His Principles

Man, of My Nightmare

Ramsey's Bed is Never Cold

Walking Crooked with Christ

Sitting on the Fence

FIND ME ON SOCIAL MEDIA

Website: SHENELLINC.COM
Facebook: Author She Nell
Twitter: AuthorShe_Nell
Instagram: authorshe_nell
Amazon: amazon.com/author/she.nell